This book is a work of fiction caused by my vivid imagination. All names, characters, events, places, products etc. have been used for this fictional purpose. If, by chance, they or it resembles someone or something; living or dead, it is by coincidence. All scriptures are taken from the Bible and is not the work of the author.

***** Although this is Christian Fiction, there is some foul language included. *****

Published by: Twins Write 2 Publishing

Last Call

Dedication

This book, like the rest, is dedicated to all of you who continue to believe in me. Please don't stop. Your encouragement and support are the fuel I need to keep writing!

My Thanks

As always, I must first thank God who is the CEO of my life. He has entrusting me with such an amazing gift and every second, I'm grateful He loves this girl enough to continually bless.

To my family; my husbae Willie, children, mom, sisters, brothers–the entire freaking family; know that I love each of you for supporting me.

A special shout out to my sister Laquisha and my girl, Shakendria who willingly helps to push out great books. You ladies rock!

To each of you who support Lakisha, the PreacHER, Author and Blogger ... THANK YOU! I wouldn't be who I am without supporters like you who purchase, download, recommend and review my books.

Please, don't stop believing in me .... THANK YOU!

Last Call

The time when customers, in a place where drinks are sold (such as a bar) are told they can order one more drink before it closes.

In life, it's when you're fed up and a decision must be made ... **Should I Stay, or Should I Go?**

Lillie

2016

"Babe, are we really doing this?"

"Blair, this is what we've been working for. Everything we have has been put into opening this bar. Sweat, tears, money, promises and sacrifices; this is what our struggle together created. It is what you want, right?"

"Lillie, it's all I've ever wanted," he says grabbing me.

I squeal as he spins me around.

"I'm so proud of you Mr. Weaver and tomorrow at 4 PM, when we cut the ribbon on this place, you'll be an official business owner."

"No, we'll be because Mrs. Weaver, I couldn't have done this without you. You've sacrificed so much for my dream and now, it's here. Right here in my hands. I'm so excited," he dances.

"I only pray you're a better business owner than you are dancer."

"Ha, ha very funny."

"Promise me something B," I say once he's done celebrating.

"Anything."

"Promise me you won't change."

"Babe–"

"No, I'm serious. The Bible says, the love of money is the root of all evil and I don't want anything to happen to us because I love the way we are. Promise me that will not change. I don't care how much money we make or the businesses we open after this, promise you'll still be the same man I married four years ago. The man who doesn't mind that I'm not materialistic or flashy. The man who loves me, the way I am and doesn't try to change me. The man who will put his family first. The man who dreams for the both of us and not just him. Promise you'll remain this man."

"I promise."

"And you'll always love me? Even if I happen to gain a little weight and my hair turns gray?"

"Always. I promise to love, honor, cherish, laugh with you, break bread with you, build businesses with you, create chocolate babies with you and make this money with you; all the days of my life until death we should part."

"Then by the power vested in me–"

"Hush woman and kiss me."

When he releases me, I smile and wipe the lip gloss from his lips.

"Babe, I promise. I'm here with you always and that will not change. Do you remember why we're naming this place B Squared? Two, spiritually, represents harmony, balance, consideration and love. I want this place to always be filled with love, but I also hope it keeps us harmonized and balanced," he says.

"I hear you but two can also mean division. However, if we work together, respect and honor what we each bring separately that builds us collectively, we'll stay balanced."

"Girl, I love you," he tells me.

"I love you too, now let's toast."

Blair grabs a bottle of champagne while I rinse out two glasses.

He pours, we raise them, and I speak, "here's to God's blessing, love and the road we've traveled thus far. God, may we always place you first in our life while you continually bless the work of our hands, marriage and B Squared Bar."

Lillie

June 2019

"Lillie! Lillie, wake up. I know you don't sleep that hard."

I let out a long breath. "Why are you yelling?" I ask looking at the clock.

"Did you get my clothes from the cleaners?" Blair, my husband yells.

"Yes, they are in your closet where they always are. Now, stop yelling."

"No, they aren't. Damn, can you do anything right?"

I sigh before throwing the comforter back and getting up. Stumping over to his closet, I open the door and grab the bag. "Dude, here. Why are you up so early, anyway?"

"I have a meeting at the office, not like it's any of your business."

"Whatever Blair. Have a great day and turn the light off."

"When your ass gets a job maybe you will understand waking up early," he spats, "instead of sleeping all day."

"Negro, I know you didn't go there. I had a job, remember? One that I loved, and you were the one who wanted me to quit."

"That's when I thought you'd make a good housewife but we both know that isn't the case."

"Okay," I laugh.

"You know I'm right."

"Yes, you're always right. Now, finish getting dressed and turn off the light. I need to sleep the rest of the day," I sarcastically say before getting back in bed. "Oh, but if I'm such a lousy wife then by all means, use the door."

"Don't tempt me."

"That's not what tempting is, business man, this is speaking facts. I'm so tired of hearing the same thing every time you're in a mood and I'm over it. If you aren't happy with the current conditions of your life, you can change them because I won't keep putting up with your demeaning of me. I don't deserve it."

"You'll put up with whatever I say you will, seeing I'm the one providing. And it isn't demeaning if it's true. Hell, I wouldn't have anything to complain about if you'd lose some weight, fix yourself up and learn how to keep a house. Until then, you'll deal with this."

"Who are you?" I question. "You can't be the same man I married and the father of the son I gave birth too, not even six months ago."

"Maybe I'm not," he pauses, "the father."

"Wow. Look Blair, I don't know what has gotten into you lately, but you need to go on and leave me alone before you talk yourself out of something you'll regret losing. You do know the tongue has power to put things into motion, right?"

"Well the only thing my tongue has gotten me is a lazy, fat, nappy headed wife. So, whatever your Bible told you is a lie. We, as in us, we have the power and if you don't shape up, the only motion my tongue will be putting out is a divorce."

I pull the comforter over me.

"Hello, cupcake got your tongue," he claps his hands.

Sighing, I move the comforter back. "Dude call me what you want but it isn't like I got myself a prize either. As I've made perfectly clear, if you aren't happy, go because I won't chase you, that's for sure."

"Says the woman I found in a little dingy ass café in that little country town in Mississippi?"

"Oh, the same place that kept you fed while you were in school, most of the time free of charge. Okay Mr. High and Mighty. Don't allow where you are now to give you amnesia about where you came from because you weren't always this," I tell him waving my hand up and down his body. "You came from nothing too and you didn't find me, boo. I wasn't lost. What you need to find is time to read your Bible and learn, *whoever keeps his mouth and his tongue keeps himself out of trouble*. Proverbs twenty-one and twenty-three."

"Yeah and you had nothing when you met me. Tell the truth and shame the devil. Grandma one and one."

"You didn't either," I yell. "You are where you are, now, because of us. I don't know what fantasy world you're living in, but you need to wake up."

"The fact remains, without me, you'll have nothing," he says grabbing his suit jacket.

"Keep thinking I can't make it without you and you might just find you're the one not needed."

He rolls his eyes. "Don't wait up."

"Had no plans too."

*****

Two hours later, I walk into the nursery.

"Look who's up and waiting on mommy," I say to BJ who is cooing in his crib. I pick him up and carry him over to the changing station. Taking off his pajamas and pamper, I walk into the bathroom that is attached to his room and run some water in the sink.

After his bath and getting him dressed, I sit in the rocking chair to nurse him. When he latches, I begin to think back on the earlier years of Blair and I's relationship. We were excited to start a family and having Blair Jr. was the most amazing feeling for me. Lately, Blair has been throwing shots like I cannot manage to live without him. I don't know what his issue is, but he's grown, and I am not in the business of raising or trying to change a grown man.

My watch notifies me of a text message. I wait until I'm done feeding and burping the baby before I get my phone from the bedroom. Putting BJ in his swing, I open the text app.

HAZEL: You are beautiful, you are whole, and God has perfected His purpose within you. No matter what you face know this, you are enough. Love you.

ME: (crying emoji) You don't know how bad I needed this. I love you too.

HAZEL: God's timing is always perfect. Are you okay?

ME: Blair ... need I say more.

HAZEL: What has the MFER done now? No, don't tell me because I'll beat the windows out of his car. Forget him. What do you need?

ME: LOL! I'm good girl. Just having a moment but I'm about to pray and leave it alone.

HAZEL: My old self has been crucified with Christ. It is no longer I who live, but Christ lives in me. So, I live in this earthly body by trusting in the Son of God, who loved me and gave himself for me. Galatians 2:20.

HAZEL: What you're going through is because of flesh. Align your thoughts with God and He'll give you what you need.

ME: Thank you and I plan to do just that.

I close my eyes and lean my head back. "God, your will and not mine. Give me the strength to win this fleshly war by the spirit, for I know God, this battle is not mine. Have your way, God. Lead me down the path you've created and whatever your will is, I'll obey. Amen."

Blair

I walk into the office and slam the door.

"Dang, what's wrong with you? It's too early to have an attitude."

"Don't start, I'm not in the mood."

"Oh," she laughs, "another fight with the wife?"

I turn to look at her and she laughs.

"Don't take your problems out on me. I've told you how this can be fixed."

"Kim, please," I state. "I need to get ready for this meeting with the folks from Limited Vodka and I can't do that with you in my ear."

"Then do what I told you. Look babe, the only reason you have this meeting is because of me. I've gotten you more business in the last three months and what do I have to show for it?"

"A paycheck," I reply, and she rolls her eyes. "You seem to forget that you're an employee."

"Sweetie, there isn't an employee on the payroll who does what I do. But you keep going home to that little, well she ain't little but you know what I mean," she says waving her hand. "Anyway, if she can't help you build then what are you there for?"

"She's my wife."

"And she can easily be your ex-wife," she adds walking out.

I sit at my desk and open my computer.

Maybe she's right.

I open the web browser and search 'Apartment Homes in Collierville'.

Thirty minutes later, Kim comes back.

"Are you ready?"

"Yeah," I tell her standing.

She walks over to fix my tie.

"Look, I'm sorry about earlier but I only want what's best for you. B Squared is eight months away from turning three years old and it's doing exceptionally well. I don't want to see you ruin that. There's so much more you can be doing."

"I know but we can finish this later. Right now, we have business to tend too and I need to be on my A game."

Two hours later, I walk the representatives out. Returning to the front of the bar, Kim is standing there in her underwear and two glasses of champagne.

"Shall we celebrate?"

*****

– I walk to the door of the nursery and hear Lillie humming. I push the door open and she quickly wipes the tears that are falling before putting the baby in his crib.

"Good morning," she states passing me, "did you bring the newspaper in with you."

"Whatever. I'm not about to argue with you."

"Who's arguing? It's after five in the morning and I've been up with your son who's teething. Yet, you don't have the decency to call or text to let your wife know you're okay or to ask if we are."

"I told you not to wait up. That's on you if you did."

"Wow," she says.

"What do you want from me?" I ask but she doesn't say anything. I grab her arm. "You don't hear me talking to you? See, this is part of the problem, you don't know your place."

She pushes me away, hard enough that I stumble back into the wall.

"I don't know what has gotten into you lately, but if you ever grab me like that again, I'll punch you in the face. I know my place and that's beside my husband, but I'll be damned if I give you respect that's not returned. Either you fix whatever it is you're going through, or I won't have any problem blessing you with the deuces."

I laugh. "Here we go again with this crap."

"Yes, here we go again because I don't know how much longer I can deal with this. You've turned into somebody I'm having a hard time recognizing. Has success made you forget everything?"

"The only thing I want–never mind," I tell her. "I'm over this conversation."

"No, please say it. You act like you're doing me a favor by showing up or taking care of me when the money that's deposited is from a business, we both own. Covering your household bills isn't taking care of me."

"Right," I laugh, "how else would they get paid? If I recall, only one of us works."

"You sound like a broken record that keeps scratching and I'm sick of it. I'm not working now because this is what WE," she yells, "agreed on. I worked my ass off to help us get here and you keep forgetting that."

"No, what I wish I could forget is the way you look right now. You lay up on your ass all day and still, I come home to you with this thing on your head," I swat at her bonnet. "The least you can do is fix yourself up."

"Fix myself up? For who? A husband who shows up at dawn and always has something negative to say? A husband who doesn't appreciate his wife and neither has he made love to said wife in over seven months, no thank you."

"I wouldn't have anything negative to speak about, if you didn't give it to me. And I come home late because I run a freaking bar. Maybe you'd know the work it takes if you ever showed up sometimes. As for making love, I'm not interested."

She laughs. "That didn't hurt like you thought it would because you aren't appealing to my senses either and I know what it takes because I've been there since the beginning. Oh, but how quickly we forget. You begged me to stop working at the clinic when the bar began making money, but I didn't because of this."

"Because of what?"

"You constantly bringing up the things you're supposed to do as a husband. Blair, I kept working until having our son, then you begged me to stay home. I DID! I've been raising him, keeping this house and the bar going for almost seven months. It was only three months ago that we hired the accounting firm to handle payroll and expenses and Kim to handle the distributors, to lessen my load. You didn't seem to have a problem with it then, why now?"

"I didn't think you'd stop supporting me. You act like you don't even care about B Squared anymore. When was the last time you offered insight to take the bar to the next level?"

"Are you serious? Negro, I worked two jobs to help you open and keep B Squared before it became profitable. I'm the one who was there nailing down floors and painting walls when the doors first opened because we couldn't afford help. I was the one who cleaned bathrooms, washed dishes and shit. Me! Or did you forget that too? I put in the work and yet every time you open your mouth lately, it's to tear me down. I don't deserve this. As for taking the bar to the next level, that's what we pay Kim Prather for, is it not?"

"Whatever, I'm not about to argue with you."

"I'm not arguing with you either, but you need to respect me. If you can't do that then maybe you can train the chick you were with tonight to do it better."

"I wasn't with anybody."

"Yeah, well tell her to change her perfume because it's funky. Maybe you'd smell it if you got your head out your ass."

I sniff my shirt and shrug.

"If I'm that bad, why do you stay?" I ask her.

"I've been asking myself and God that question a lot lately. I can tell you this, I don't know how much more I can take."

"Maybe you'll get the answer sooner than later."

"What does that mean?" she asks but I walk into the bathroom and slam the door.

The next morning, I pull into the new apartment building near Collierville.

"Good afternoon sir, may I help you?"

"I was wondering if you have any two-bedroom apartments available. I'm looking for something that is move-in ready."

"Sure. My name is Abigail."

"Blair Weaver," I reply taking her hand.

"Mr. Weaver, we have a few apartments available that I can show you. Is there a preference of floor level and would you like a garage?"

"Yes, to the garage and a first floor, if you have one," I tell her.

She grabs an iPad. "Um, yes I have one. I'll need to make a copy of your driver's license then I can give you a tour."

Forty-five minutes later, we walk back into the leasing office. "I hope the apartment exceeds your expectation Mr. Weaver."

"It does, and I'd like to go ahead and fill out the paperwork. How soon can I take possession?"

"Once you're done with the paperwork, I'll run all the necessary credit checks and I should have an answer within a few hours. If you're approved–"

"When," I correct her. "When I'm approved."

"My apologies. There's a $65 application fee and when you're approved, you'll pay the first month rent and deposit and you can take possession in two days or less."

"Perfect. What about the electric and water?"

"The water and electric will remain on for three days, to give you time to transfer them into your name."

"Where do I sign?"

Lillie

I walk into Haze, a restaurant owned by my best friend Hazel Russell and she is yelling like usual.

"Girl, all that screaming can cause a stroke," I say from behind her.

"Hey," she says hugging me. "Sister, it seems screaming is the only way to get things done right. Miguel, you must make sure that steak is cooked to perfection every time. Charlie–"

"I know Hazel," he says before she can continue her rant.

She rolls her eyes. "What are you doing here?" she asks pulling me into another hug. "I feel like I haven't seen you in forever."

"You just saw me a week ago," I laugh. "Anyway, I needed some adult time, so I took the baby to Ms. Laura's for a few hours."

"Let's go to my office and you can tell me what's really going on with you and Blair."

"I think he's cheating," I tell her once we're inside. "Ever since I had the baby, he's been making snide remarks about my weight, my hair and the way I keep the house. Hazel, he's gotten so nasty and the time he comes home is getting later and later."

"Um, first, nothing is wrong with you and don't you let that simpleminded bastard put negative thoughts in your mind. Second, he can only do to you what you accept."

"Believe me, I'm confident in who I am. God made me and all this, in His glory. Besides, I've been called worse by better and made it through; I'll make it this time too. With or without him. As for accepting this behavior, you're right but I don't know how much longer I will."

"What are you going to do?" she inquires.

"I'm going to do what I've always done, take care of me and now, BJ."

"Well, you know I am here for you."

"I know," I say with tears in my eyes. "Do you know he had the nerve to tell me, the other night, I don't support him or care about the bar?"

"Are you freaking serious? Lillie, that bar wouldn't be open had it not been for you. You sacrificed time, money and your sanity to make sure Blair's dream became a reality."

I cover my face.

"No, don't you cry over him. He isn't worth your tears."

"I know but it hurts to hear him say the things he does. It's like I don't even know who he is anymore. In the last year, he's turned into a monster."

She comes over to me. "Money has the ability to do that to some people. But Lillie, this is going to hurt because you love him and have been building a life with the person he used to be. However, you must decide if the person he is now, is the one you want to continue with. My grandmother always told me, if a person can't appreciate your presence, make them appreciate your absence."

"Hazel, I know what I've put into him, this marriage and that bar but it was because of God blessing us."

"And your obedience. Girl don't discount the power we women have, especially as wives. Why do you think I'm not out here playing in these streets? God made us to be wives because of the favor He's put into us. Proverbs nineteen and fourteen says, *houses and wealth are inherited from fathers, but a wise wife is from the Lord."*

I smile at her.

"Child, those Bible study lessons are paying off," she laughs, "and if you won't say it, I will. You worked your ass off to make sure your man succeeded, and he has because of your favor, not his."

"I'm only being faithful to my assignment as his wife and I had no problem doing that for the man I married, but this new him has become all high and mighty."

"One of the ministers of our church preached on pride, a few weeks ago," she says getting up to get her phone. "She came from Proverbs twenty-nine and twenty-three that says, *"a man's pride will bring him low, but a humble spirit will obtain honor."* She said, you never have to fight those who are led by pride because just as sure as pride shows up, disgrace soon peaks its ugly head. Lillie, this isn't your battle. It doesn't mean it won't hurt less but you can't fight this and win. Give him the space to fall because he'll need you again, in this lifetime."

"Amen. Thank you," I tell her.

"You never have to thank me for being a friend. God knows you've been there for me. Lillie, I know you'll survive this because your heart is humble. Don't allow him to change that."

"I'm not perfect," I correct her.

"I didn't say you were but you're also not prideful. Lillie, you've been there for me more ways that I can count and if I can repay you a hundred times what you've given me, it still wouldn't be enough."

I stand and give her a hug.

Leaving Hazel and getting to the car, my phone rings. I start the car, lock the doors and allow it to connect to Bluetooth before answering.

"Hello."

"Hi, is this Lillian Weaver?"

"It is."

"My name is William Grant from First Horizon Bank."

"First Horizon Bank? What's going on?"

"I need to verify your social security number because the one on the application submitted isn't correct."

"Mr. Grant, I haven't filled out any application. What is this for?"

"For the business loan," he says. "The application was completed online this morning. A joint request with you and your husband, Blair Weaver."

"For how much?"

"Two hundred and fifty thousand," he replies.

"Two hundred–Mr. Grant, I'm not sure what's going on, but I haven't applied for any loan."

He grunts. "I received a copy of your driver's license and all of your information and assumed you were aware."

"I'm not. Is there not a way for you to verify who is submitting this stuff?" I question.

"Yes ma'am, of course."

"Look Mr. Grant, I'm not giving you my authorization or social security number for any loan.

However, give me your number and the address of your branch."

I grab a pen and paper from the console, jotting down his information.

"I'll call you back."

I pull into the parking lot of B Squared. Fuming, I walk through the back door and into Blair's office.

"Lillie," he says getting up from his chair, "what are you doing here?"

"I got a–" I stop when Kim walks out of his bathroom closing her shirt.

"Babe–oh, hey Lillie, I didn't know you were here?" she smirks.

"Babe? Is this what we're doing now?" I say to Blair.

"Lillie, what's up? Why are you here?" he nonchalantly asks.

"Why am I here? I own this place, is that good enough? Kim, please excuse us," I state.

"You don't have to leave," Blair tells her. "Lillie, what's up?"

I look at her and she smiles taking a seat on the couch.

"You need to leave so I can speak to my husband," I tell her.

"Your husband said I didn't have too," she shrugs her shoulders.

"Blair, you need to check your lap dog because I'm not in the mood for you or her."

"And I'm not in the mood for whatever drama you came here with. Go home and we'll talk about this later." He says waving me off.

"I'm not going anywhere until you tell me why I got a call from someone at a bank talking about a loan WE," I emphasize, "applied for."

"It's a loan. What's the problem?"

I close my eyes and take a deep breath.

"I haven't given you authority to apply for a loan in my name."

"It's the least you can do," Kim pipes up.

"Excuse you?"

"You don't do anything else for Blair, the least you can do is sign for a loan."

"And the least you can do is wear lipstick that doesn't stain your teeth. Worry about your problems and I'll handle mine." I turn back to Blair. "Now, what in the hell–"

"Even with lipstick on my teeth, I look better than you, Shirley," she laughs. "Hell, you aren't concerned with your husband or you'd be here or home fixing yourself up instead of looking like this," she waves her hand.

"Kim, that's enough," Blair yells.

"What? I'm just saying. I've been here three months and she's been here what, twice but she will call to nag, relentlessly. You've even said it yourself, boo," she says to Blair. "Sweetie, take my advice and approve the loan while I take care of everything else."

I chuckle before dropping my purse and charging at her, punching her everywhere my hand can land. Blair struggles to pull us apart.

"Lillie stop, what are you doing?"

He lets me go and I punch him before grimacing in pain.

"I'm doing what your dog ass couldn't. Putting this bitch in her place. How dare you think I'm going to stand and allow someone we pay to disrespect me. I've let you slide long enough."

"You don't pay me," she screams, "and you better hope I don't press charges."

I flinch, grabbing her wig. When it comes off, leaving her looking like a mannequin head, she yelps and runs into the bathroom.

"Lillie, damn, will you stop acting a fool. You bust my lip," he says walking over to his desk. "Yes, I applied for a loan because I need it to purchase a new building. Had you been more supportive or in tune with everything going on, you'd know that. Instead, you pick and choose when to support me."

"Negro, you not having to do a damn thing at home is supporting you. When was the last time you've been supportive of me? I give you the space to run this bar without any problems, I never say anything about the amount of money you spend nor the time I rarely see you and now you want to act like you're doing me a favor? Well fuck you and this duck with red lipstick on her teeth."

"All I'm saying is, you need to be a better wife," he casually states.

"A better wife? Dude, who do you think kept this bar in the black until it started making money? It sure wasn't you. You're only at this point because of the favor on my life, not yours."

"Man don't start all that Bible stuff with me. I'm where I am because of me."

"Great, then you don't need me. Let your minion get the loan or here's a thought, get it yourself."

Blair

I pick up Kim's wig and open the bathroom door. "She's gone," I say when she jumps. Looking in the mirror, I grab a towel and wet it to put to my lip.

"Damn it," I yell throwing the towel. "She's going to ruin everything. I need her signature on that loan."

"Then make her do it."

"She's a grown woman Kim, I can't make her do anything. Did you not just see her?"

"Yeah and I also felt that big heifer. Hell, I think she snatched out some of my edges," she states fixing her hair. "Blair, you can't let her ruin this."

"What am I supposed to do? She's definitely not going to sign it now that she knows about us."

"Stop whining," she says turning to me. "Here's what you do. In a few hours, order some takeout, stop and get her favorite bottle of wine and go home. Apologize for the way you treated her, tell her you put me in my place for the disrespect and let her think you've talked me out of pressing charges. After she's had a couple glasses of wine, begin to massage her and when she's comfortable screw her good. You'll need to give her more than one orgasm, tire her out and then later when she asks, pretend the loan is no big deal."

"That won't work. She isn't dumb and will see right through it. I'm supposed to suddenly act like I care. Nah, there has to be another way."

She snatches my face.

"Man up. Hell, your wife has more balls than you right now. Blair, whatever you must promise her, do it but make sure her name is first. Once we have the second location of B Squared open, we'll let her take the fall for the payments."

We walk back into the office.

"Oh, Abigail from the apartments called. You were approved, and she needs you to sign the lease and pick up the keys."

"Great."

"See, I told you everything will work out. All you have to do is trust me."

*****

"Thank you, Abigail. You've been a great help."

"You're welcome Mr. Weaver. Here are the keys and you can officially move in tomorrow. Like I stated before, the lights and water will be on for the next three days. If you need more time to get everything transferred, call and let me know. Do you have any questions for me?"

"Nope."

"Great. You're in building 18 and apartment 102. Here's my card. If you have any problems or questions, don't hesitate to call."

I take the paperwork, keys and gate openers and leave out smiling.

An hour later, I'm walking in the house and drop the bag of food on the counter. I snatch the refrigerator open, mad that I've come home, and Lillie isn't even here. I slam the door and go into the bedroom. After showering and throwing on some jogging pants and t-shirt, I lay across the bed.

I open my eyes when I hear water running in the bathroom. By the time Lillie opens the door, I'm sitting on the side of the bed. She walks pass me.

"Hello to you too," I say getting up.

She keeps on into the closet.

"Lillie, I'm talking to you."

"And I could give a flying flip, get out of my face," she says.

"Can we please talk?"

"Talk?" she laughs. "Now you want to talk? Nah pooh, I'll pass. Go back and talk to Lil Bertha."

"Lil Bertha?"

"That's what Kim looks like without her wig," she says before throwing on an oversize shirt. I follow her into the kitchen.

"I brought us dinner."

"Save it, I'd rather eat out the garbage."

"Babe, I know you're upset and if you don't want to talk, just listen. Please Lillie. I need to apologize for today."

"Just today. Dude, you could talk to three in the morning and it'll never be enough to make up for whoever this is you've become. I don't even know you anymore."

I walk to where she is and grab her hands.

"I'm the same person you married and I'm sorry for allowing things between us to get out of hand. Lillie, I love you and our son, and I don't want to lose you."

"You have a funny way of showing it," she says snatching away. "You allow your little girlfriend to disrespect me and now you think bringing home takeout, is going to fix everything. It won't."

"She's not my girlfriend and I put her in her place as soon as you left. I also talked her out of pressing charges."

"I don't care about any of that because you should have put her in her place then fired her, while I was there. As a matter of fact, you never should have given her the authority to think she could disrespect me in the first place. There's no going back from that. I'm fighting like some street savage and I'm ashamed of what I've allowed you to turn me into. I'm tired Blair and quite frankly I think this thing with us is nearing last call."

"Last call," I repeat confused.

"Yeah, you know how you make the last call at the bar, signifying closing time is approaching; well we're getting there in this marriage because I'm sick of putting up with you and your shit. You got the audacity to treat me like I'm nothing when I've been with you since you couldn't afford Vienna Sausages and crackers, at the same time. We struggled together and with God, it produced everything we have now. Instead of you seeing the blessing, you're too busy bragging and I want no parts of this."

"Baby, I know I've messed things up but please give me another chance to make things right. Whatever it'll take I'll do it, but I need you."

"No, you need me to sign that freaking loan. I'm not stupid Blair and you standing in my face, acting, shows just how little you think of me. If anybody should know me, it's you but apparently you've forgotten."

"That's not true. I don't care about the loan, I need to make things right with us. Seeing that side of you made me realize how wrong I've been and I'm sorry. I've made a mess of all we've worked for."

"Seeing that side of me was for the principle of respect, not you. It's one thing to tolerate the crap from you, but when you allow someone else to blatantly do it, I know it's time we call this what it is."

"What's that?"

"Over. I've stayed longer than I should have. Tomorrow, I'm going to the bank and I'm taking my name off B Squared. This was always your dream anyway, I was just too stupid to think you wanted me in it."

"No baby, please don't say that. I'm sorry but you can't give up on us." I move to kiss her, but she backs away. "Lillie, you are a part of this."

"Yeah, and it's purely a coincidence that you're sorry and saying the right things the same day William Grant calls from First Horizon needing my social security number."

"Damn Lillie, I'm here trying to make things right but you're making it hard to love you."

"Wow, really? How? By demanding the respect I'm supposed to get from my husband? You haven't had a nice word to say to me, in months and now because you need my credit and good name; I'm supposed to believe the shit coming from your mouth. I don't, and just so you know, you're not easy to love either but I never would have given up on you like you've done me."

She passes me and heads toward our bedroom. A few minutes later, I walk in to see her stuffing clothes in a bag.

"What are you doing?"

"Not this," she says. "Not anymore."

"Baby stop," I place my hands on hers. "This isn't going how I planned. Give me a chance to apologize."

She sighs before sitting on the bed and I kneel in front of her.

"Yes, I've fucked up these past six months and I don't have an excuse for it. I've neglected you, our son, this house and I'm sorry. I've allowed my desire of making the bar successful to let my home suffer. Please forgive me."

"Love shouldn't be this hard Blair. Yes, I get that we'll have our ups and downs but come on, it shouldn't be like this. Every day you look at me like I disgust you. What happened to you cherishing and honoring me? Do you not realize I'm your favor? I'm supposed to be your good thing, yet you treat me like garbage."

I wipe the tears that are falling from her eyes.

"Please don't cry."

She slaps my hand away. "Don't. You can't wipe the tears you caused without giving me a reason to believe you won't make me cry again. Your words and actions cut deep, and I don't deserve it. I've never done anything but support you, even when I shouldn't have. I've been here and the time we should be celebrating the blessings of God, you're acting like this is all because of you."

She tries to stand up, but I wrap my arms around her waist.

"Give me a chance to fix this."

"This isn't a flat tire, it's my life and I'm tired. I can't live like this anymore. Your son deserves better. Hell, I deserve better."

"I know and I'm trying to fix it," I reply raising up to kiss her lips. She tries to push me away. "Baby, please. I need you," I whine kissing her again. "It's been too long since I've felt your skin against mine." I kiss her neck. "Please baby," I kiss her chest and she moans. "Please," I say again this time covering her mouth with mine. She hesitates but allows me to kiss her.

"Please," I whisper.

She wraps her hand around my neck before allowing me to remove her shirt.

Lillie

The next morning, I open my eyes and jump when I see Blair sleeping next to me. Looking over at the clock, it's 8:22 AM. I get up and go into the bathroom and after brushing my teeth, washing and moisturizing my face, I turn the water on for the shower. Grabbing my phone, I connect it to the speakers and *Nothing Even Matters* by *Lauryn Hill* begins to play.

I start swaying and singing to the music.

"Now the skies could fall, not even if my boss should call. The world it seems so very small cause nothing even matters, at all. See nothing even matters. See nothing' even matters at all. Nothing even matters. Nothing even matters at all. See, I don't need no alcohol, your love makes me feel ten feet tall. Without it, I'd go through withdrawal Cause nothing' even matters at all."

As the song continues, tears fall.

I jump when I feel Blair's hands touch me.

"Babe," he says.

"When did I stop mattering to you?"

"You haven't. Everything that has happened is because of me, not you."

"But it doesn't stop the pain coursing through me each time my heart beats. You're the only man I've loved this way and I used to feel like nothing else mattered because your love made me feel ten feet tall. Now, I feel like I'm not worth the dirt on your shoes." I step away from him. "Just go Blair. Please."

The song continues. "You're part of my identity. I sometimes have the tendency to look at you religiously, baby cause nothing even matters to me."

He turns me to face him and he has tears falling too.

"I love you Lillian Shantay Weaver and I'd die without you. Please forgive me and give me a chance to make things right."

"I love you too but it's too late."

I remove my gown and get in the shower.

The music changes to *Stay* by *Tyrese* and he begins to sing, horribly.

"Yeah, girl I wanna take the time and thank you. Just for putting up with me and I'm sorry, that you even had to deal with me. Even though I made you cry, I wanna make it right. Just give me some time to make it right. I'll go the extra mile to make you smile and just to make your day. I'll go out my way I'll do whatever it takes. Baby promise you'll stay. Stay baby."

He gets into the shower with me.

After Blair leaves and getting BJ settled, I go about cleaning the house. A few hours later, I get a call from Mr. Grant. I ignore it.

I sit on the couch and open my text message.

ME: Why do you really need this loan?

HUSBAND: Babe, you don't have to worry about the loan.

ME: Why do you need the loan Blair?

HUSBAND: B Squared is doing well and I know if we open a much larger one downtown, it's going to be even better.

ME: We?

He calls. I put the phone on speaker. Yes, you and me. Lillie, I know I couldn't have open B Squared without you and I apologize for even saying that. We're what we are today because of you. However, if you don't want to be in on the new bar, I'll find another way.

"I'll think about it," I tell him.

"You will?"

"Yeah, but I want to talk to Mr. Grant first. I'm going to go by the bank and I'll let you know."

"Thank you and Lillie, I love you."

"I love you too."

I lay the phone down, "God, I need you to guide me because I'll mess things up on my own. Show me what you'll have me to do. Don't allow me to be led by flesh but by your favor. I love my husband, but I love you more. Please open my eyes, ears, direct my heart and my path. Thank you, God, and amen."

After getting me and the baby dressed, I head to First Horizon.

"Mrs. Weaver, thank you for coming in."

"Mr. Grant, let's chat."

Later that evening, I walk into Mount Carmel for Bible study.

"Good evening Mount Carmel, I pray your week, thus far has been great." Pastor Wyatt says. "We're going to get right into the lesson tonight as it's a topic I've been getting a lot of questions on. Tonight, we're going to discuss mental soul ties.

Pastor Wyatt

"Soul, S-O-U-L means the spiritual part of a human being, the emotional or intellectual energy or intensity. Spiritually, the soul is the very breath of God that He blows into each of us to give life. Bible says in Genesis two and seven, *"And the LORD God formed man of the dust of the ground and breathed into his nostrils the breath of life; and man became a living soul."*

Now, a tie T-I-E, the verb tense, means to attach or fasten someone or something with a string or cord, to restrict or limit, to connect or link. Tie, noun tense, means a thing that unites or links people. Therefore, if by merging these 2 definitions, a soul tie is something that's fastened to your soul that can potentially restrict or limit you.

However, here's what you need to understand, the Bible doesn't mention soul ties, the same as it doesn't mention soul mates but that's another discussion.

And this may hurt your feelings, to hear and may even be hard to swallow but soul ties aren't a biblical thing, they're flesh. Yet, we try to make them spiritual but if you search the Bible, you won't find it.

I know you're wondering, why is this thing, mental soul ties, a biblical lesson. It's because too many of us use the crutch of soul ties as to why we can't break stuff off. Well beloved, here's the reality of your situation. You're mentally tied to some stuff, that's true but it's because you like the way it looks even though you know it's temporary. Your mental is tied to that thang that looks good but ain't worth nothing if you were to remove the nice suit, wig, makeup, leggings and grey sweat pants. But you stay connected to it because it's comfortable.

Some of you have stayed in relationship with soul ties because you don't want to be like your momma and daddy who divorced. Or maybe it's because folk look up to you and you're embarrassed to admit it didn't work. Some of you won't uncuff yourself from mental soul ties, even though you know they aren't good for your sanity and you're holding the key.

Your situation-ship is affecting your mental when you know good and well, it can only give you a natural orgasm for momentary excitement but nothing long term. It can make you feel good with your eyes closed and your body naked but can't do nothing when you're standing up and clothed.

Bible shares in Romans twelve, verses one and two, *"Therefore I urge you, brethren, by the mercies of God, to present your bodies a living and holy sacrifice, acceptable to God, which is your spiritual service of worship. And do not be conformed to this world, but be transformed by the renewing of your mind, so that you may prove what the will of God is, that which is good and acceptable and perfect."*

However, most of us conform because the mental soul ties have altered your perception of reality. You don't think you can do any better because the person you're tied too toys with your mental. They know you don't do well with loss, so they keep threatening to leave. They play games with your mind because they remember you saying, you don't want to raise your children in a broken home. They know you got daddy

issues, so they string you along making you believe nobody else will want you. The promises they made, they could care less about breaking them or you and you keep putting up with it, hoping they change. Destroy the ties.

How do you know if you have mental soul ties? It changes your mental health and I don't mean for the good. How do you know if your mental is tied to something no good? It changes your mood and alters your thinking. How do you know if you are the victim of mental soul ties? You can't think for yourself, you act out of character around the one who's pulling the strings and you don't ever see what everybody else does.

This is why people will say, you act differently when you're around so and so or when you go to certain places. How do you know what or who your mental soul tie is? It's that person, place or thing that can change your perception of everything, your attitude and your character. Destroy the ties.

Romans eight and five says, "For those who live according to the flesh set their minds on the things of the flesh, but those who live according to the Spirit, the things of the Spirit." What does this mean? In simplistic terms, when we live of the flesh, we desire things that satisfies our flesh. But how many of you know, things of the flesh are what man can take, break, destroy and bind us with.

However, when we live according to the spirit, we produce fruit of the spirit. Galatians five, twenty-two and twenty-three, "But the fruit of the Spirit is love, joy, peace, patience, kindness, goodness, faithfulness, gentleness, self-control; against such things there is no law." There is no law against being loving, peaceful, joyful etc.

Now, the fruit of the flesh is the opposite. It's lust, hopelessness, pain, impatience, anger, no compassion, rough, no self-control and there isn't a faithful bone in your body. Unless it's being faithful to breaking promises, hurting folk etc. These things, there are laws because each of these emotions can lead us to do things that can hurt others. Destroy the ties."

"How do you destroy the ties?" someone questions.

"Yeah, if they aren't spiritual, how do you destroy them?"

"By destroying it," I chuckle. "Seriously, the only way you can destroy it, you have to DESTROY IT," I say the last part slowly. "Come here Sister Lester. I went to Goodwill and I purchased some old ties," I tell them placing one around her wrist. "Stand right there for me."

I pause for a second. "When you're mentally tied to something or someone you think about them constantly. What are they doing? Who are they with? What do they have on? What do they smell like? Why? Look at Sister Lester," I tell them. "For as long as she's had that tie around her wrist, she's played with it. Why?" I ask her.

"It's there," she shrugs.

"Exactly. It's a part of you. Now, if I remove it and lay it here, Sister Lester can pick it up and put it back on. But if I destroy it," I take a pair of scissors and begin to cut it up then I hand her a piece.

"Try to tie that to you."

"I can't," she tells me, "it's too small."

"Just maybe if it's too small to tie to you, it'll be the right size for you to forget it. People of God destroy the tie by cutting it off, up, out or whatever you have to do. Maybe you can't cut it up, but you can move. See, sometimes our mental can be tied to a person or place because we're still staying where the abuse happened. We're living where we know the pain occurred. We're sleeping in the same bed the person who vowed to love you but didn't used to sleep. Come back one last time, Sister Lester." I tie another tie around her wrist and the other end to mine. Then I walk out as far as I can. "I can only go as far as this will allow me to go," I cut it, "until I destroy the tie.

Galatians five and one says, *"Stand fast therefore in the liberty by which Christ has made us free, and do not be entangled again with a yoke of bondage."* Let's break this scripture down." I go over to the flip chart that I wrote this scripture on earlier and get a marker. "Liberty is freedom or authority." I scratch out the word and write the meaning.

"Entangled means to have within, to hold in, to be engaged with, set one's self against or to hold a grudge against. I'm not going to write all those words, but you get it. Yoke, Y-O-K-E, biblically here means, use of any burden and bondage is bondage. In other words, God has set us free so why are we holding on to something or someone we've given the authority to burden us. They only have the power we give them. Why are we holding grudges against folk who have done us wrong? Why are we continually getting angry over what they did instead of forgiving them and moving on?"

"Maybe because we need closure," someone says.

"Why do you need closure? What peace can closure give you that leaving can't? Let's be honest with self on tonight. Some of you, if you see the person who hurt you, you'll get fighting mad. If you hear their name, your blood boils. Scroll past a post about them on Facebook and you start mumbling to yourself. So, I ask again. Why do you need closure before you can destroy the mental tie you allowed to be created?

Closure is sometimes needed, don't get me wrong, but trying to get healing from the person who left you wounded, don't always end well because they might not know how to give you what you want. Forgive them, even if you only speak it to the wind and make right the offense you caused. But that apology, it may never come and while you're waiting, your mental is being tormented.

Destroy the tie. Romans fourteen and nineteen says, "Therefore let us pursue the things which make for peace and the things by which one may edify another." Any questions?" I poll the congregation.

"If there's anything you think of later, submit it to the church's email address and I'll answer them on next week. If there's nothing more, let's pray. Dear God, thank you. Thank you for giving us another chance, another minute of your grace and another day to bask in your glory. Now God, I ask that you forgive us. Forgive us for holding on to the ties that are disturbing our mental. Forgive us for holding grudges instead of forgiving those who hurt us.

Forgive us for taking your peace for granted. Father, tonight I ask you to strengthen every man and woman who's listening, with the courage to destroy the ties.

Not just mental but physical, emotional, social, financial, sexual and even spiritual ties. Give us the strength to destroy what we gave power to stay. No more shall we live with the burdens of broken promises and hearts. No more will we live with the hurt and shame. What's done is done and we can't change it, but we can move on from it. Tonight Father, allow us to leave this place freer than we were when we came in. Give us the words to forgive and the boldness to bask in the effects of being released from bondage. We thank you father and until we shall all gather again, keep us. Amen."

Blair

I hang up the phone. "It worked, oh my God," I laugh. "Oh my God, it actually worked. You're a genius. That was Mr. Grant."

"I told you," Kim says sitting in my lap and wrapping her arms around my neck. "Now, why don't you thank me by removing these pants."

A few hours later, after taking a shower at Kim's, I'm redressed.

"Where are you going?" she asks sitting up in the bed.

"It's time to get the ball rolling."

"What do you mean?"

"I need to call the movers and see if they can fit me in tomorrow. Mr. Grant said he has everything he needs to finish processing the loan and the money should be deposited into my account in two days. So, there's no need on prolonging the inevitable. Once I get the movers scheduled, I'm going to contact my lawyer to release the divorce papers I had drawn up." I grab her and kiss her. "Are you ready to see what's waiting for us on the other side?"

"I sure am Mr. Weaver, but I think you need to wait until the money is actually deposited."

"Nah, I got this. The loan is processing so she can't stop it. Anyway, I'll continue to lay on the charm tonight and by the time she figures out what's happening, it'll be too late."

The next morning, after making love to Lillie again, I wait until she leaves for her standing lunch date with Hazel. I was cutting it close but thirty minutes later, the truck from Three Men and a Truck Moving pulls in front of the house.

"Right on time," I say opening the door.

"Mr. Weaver," the gentleman says.

"That's me."

"My name is Perry and we have a request to get you packed up. The order is incomplete, so I can't give you an estimate on time or cost."

"I know, it was a last-minute request but come on inside and I'll show you what's going. As for time and money, that's not a problem."

A little bit later, I hear Lillie's voice. "Blair, what is going on? I get a call from Ms. Laura saying there's a moving van at our house. What is all this?" she questions.

"This is me getting what I want. A new beginning with what makes me happy. Look Lillie, I'm sorry for things happening like this, but hey you said it right, we're nearing closing time, and this is last call," I yell then laugh. "Here," I say holding out an envelope.

"What's this?"

"Your new address," I state matter-of-factly.

"You're kicking me and your son out?"

"Call it what you like. That's the location of your new apartment, along with a gate fob and keys. I paid the first two months, for you and this nice gentleman will help you with all your things. Take whatever you like, I'll replace it." I tell her. "By the way, you're welcome."

"Hi ma'am, Lillie, oh my God, I haven't seen you in forever."

"Perry," she throws her arms around him, "how are you and Gillian?"

"Well, her cancer has returned but she's being strong as usual," he tells her.

"I'm sorry to hear that. Is she going through chemo again–"

I clear my throat. "Can you two keep the chatter to a minimum and finish this?"

Lillie rolls her eyes.

"Perry, I'm going to make sure you got everything I need and then we can get going."

Thirty minutes later, she comes into the living room where I'm kicked back with a glass of Bourbon.

"Are you done?" I question.

"You know, these last few months I've put up with a lot of your shit. From your name calling to you not coming home but I never pegged you for a coward. You claim to want better but sweetie, Bible says in Ecclesiastes six and nine, *"Enjoy what you have rather than desiring what you don't have. Just dreaming about nice things is meaningless–like chasing the wind."*

"Yeah and Bobby Womack says, it's all over now. Lillie, we've been friends since we were nineteen, in a relationship almost eleven years and married seven; it's safe to say that things have run their course. I don't have any ill feelings for you, but I want something better than what you can offer. I want a woman who looks good on my arm, who encourages and builds me. Unfortunately, it isn't you."

I wipe the tears that are falling.

"Please don't start crying. Just accept this for what it is."

"These tears aren't for you, they're for our son. I only wish you'd showed me who you really are before we created him together."

"Isn't it somewhere in your Bible about God's timing being perfect?" I laugh.

"Keep laughing at God. I only pray our son will never treat another human being as worthless as you've treated me. As a matter of fact, I'm going to make sure the remnants of narcissism that's within your blood never rest in his. I'll make sure he understands the power he possesses with his tongue and actions. You sir, I pray God will have mercy on your pitiful soul."

"I don't need your prayers. I'm good, but good luck to you," I state sitting the glass down and getting up.

"I don't need luck, I have God. You though, you need to be careful what you ask for."

"You were the one that said this was the last call, not me. I only obliged. Besides, I got this."

"Yeah, but what you don't have is a loan. Goodbye Blair."

"What did you say?" I scream but she continues out the door and over to Perry. I rush to where she is.

"What did you say?" I ask jumping in front of her.

"Oh, you didn't hear me? Well, let me say it slower and plainer. I knew you were full of shit but a small piece of me thought you were being honest and sincere. Although my heart was showing me you weren't, I was willing to give you the benefit of the doubt. So, when I went to the bank, I asked Mr. Grant to tell you everything was good with the loan and that the money would be deposited into your account in order to see the real you. Thank you. Oh, I also appreciate the few orgasms you managed to give, they weren't the best, but it'll hold me over until God sends me a real man."

"Damn," one of the movers say.

"Perry, will you give me a few minutes?" she asks before walking across the street.

"Lillie," I scream. "Lillie, get back here!"

I run back into the house, get my phone and call the bank.

"This is William Grant."

"Grant, what is going on? Where is my money?"

"Mr. Weaver, hello. Well sir, I received a call from your wife a few minutes ago telling me to remove her name."

"But you said you had everything you needed."

"Yes sir, I know what I said but I also have to have her permission and without her social security number and notarized signature; I can't proceed. Now, you still qualify, by yourself but for a quarter of the amount."

"I don't need a quarter, I need all of it."

"I'm sorry sir, but that's all I can do."

I throw the phone into the wall.

Lillie

"Perry, will you give me a few minutes?"

"Yes ma'am," he replies.

I walk over to Ms. Laura's home with Blair yelling my name. I let her know what's going on and that I'd be back to get the baby. Getting to my car, I put the address in the GPS. I get to the apartment and surprisingly it's nice with two bedrooms, each with their own bath.

Before they begin to bring my things in, I walk around the apartment praying.

"God, I come to you in humble submission and with your permission asking you to bless this space. God don't allow harm, evil, sickness, danger, lack, sleepless nights, hunger or negativity to enter here. Cover now with the blood of Jesus every square foot. Turn this apartment into a home, for the time we shall be here. And God, don't let my heart feel less than what you allow towards Blair. I thank you for the years we've spent, and I wouldn't change anything. I pray your grace over his life that he never gets what he rightfully deserves but he receives your forgiveness. Forgive him Father. I pray You'll make the plan for my life plain that I don't miss you in everything. Your plan, God, is far better than mine. Guide, lead, protect, provide and let me see you in everything. Your will God and not mine. Amen."

I turn to see Perry standing at the door with a box.

"My apologies," he states. "I didn't want to interrupt."

"No problem. This room is going to be the nursery," I tell him when I see the box in his hands.

He and his crew finish bringing in my things. Once they're done, he hands me a phone with a place to sign.

"Lillie, are you going to be okay?"

"Yes, I'm going to be just fine."

"There is no bedroom, living room or kitchen items," he says with sadness in his eyes. "What will you sleep on?"

"Perry, I've been taking care of myself for a while, I'll survive this."

"I just feel bad about leaving you like this."

"Don't be. Whatever God has planned for my life, I'll be obedient. If that means being here, now, so be it. As for furniture, I'll take care of it tomorrow. Anyway, do you have a card, in case I need your services again?"

"Yes, and I will write my cell on the back. If you need help with anything, please call."

"Will do and I'll text you, so you'll have my number as well. Tell Gillian to call me whenever she needs anything."

"I will. Take care Lillie."

I spend the night at Ms. Laura's, although I didn't sleep. I roll over, looking up at the ceiling. Closing my eyes, I begin to pray out loud. "God, thank you for this new day. Thank you for keeping your arms around me and thank you for directing my path. Father, I may not know your plans for me but have your way. Guard my heart so that it isn't harden by anger. Give me the strength to be healed because I can't do this alone. Please God, help me. Amen."

I get my phone and send an email to Mr. Grant making sure he knows there is to be nothing approved in my name unless I'm sitting face to face with him. When I'm done getting dressed; I bathed, clothed and feed BJ before heading into the kitchen, putting him on his mat. Sitting at the island, Ms. Laura places a cup of coffee in front of me.

"How are you?"

"I'm okay," I smile.

She touches my hand. "I heard you crying last night and while you cried, I prayed. Lillie, God is taking care of you. He told me, the same way He took care of you when your grandparents died, He's going to take care of you now."

I look at her.

"He told me to tell you, He's doing exactly what you asked. He's opening your eyes and guarding your heart, but you have to trust Him."

I burst into tears.

"I do trust God but I'm angry," I yell hitting the counter. "I've been everything Blair needed. Even when I didn't know how to be a wife, I prayed and studied God's word. Ms. Laura, I loved Blair the way I wanted him to love me because that's what the Bible says. In Philippians two, it says, *"do nothing from selfishness or empty conceit, but with humility of mind regard one another as more important than yourselves."* I did that," I cry, "and it was for nothing."

"Yes, you've done your part and you have a right to be angry because Blair is an asshole, who's only thinking about himself. However, don't ever think for a moment that all you've done is for nothing. When God created you, He did so with the virtue of a wife and just because Blair didn't know how to take care of God's masterpiece, it doesn't make you worthless. Your value is still yours and the only person who can diminish it is you."

"I'm angrier at me, though," I say. "I gave him permission to do this to me. For months, I've allowed him to degrade me when I know my worth. He comes and goes as he pleases while I'm home taking care of a son, he wanted. Ms. Laura, he packed up my stuff like I was a roommate he evicted for not paying rent. I'm his wife, the mother of his son and he threw me away. I was there when he had nothing."

She wraps her arms around me and I weep.

"I let him do this."

"No," she says grabbing my face. "Look at me. Don't you ever take responsibility for the actions of a selfish person. You may have stayed longer than you should but that's because you didn't want to see your family broken."

"Yet, I still left broken and it hurts," I touch my chest. "The pain feels like I'm suffocating and can't catch my breath."

"Bible shares in Job, thirty-three and four, "*the Spirit of God has made me, And the breath of the Almighty gives me life.*" Lillie, the heaviness of the weight you've been handed has you feeling like this, but with God, His breath will give you life. Even when it seems as though you can't breathe for yourself, trust that God will do it for you. For the one breath you take, God will take four. Yes, it hurts when you're broken, but you can heal. You simply have to decide how and when."

I wipe my face.

"What do you mean?" I ask her.

"You can allow this hurt to drag on or you can forgive and move on. This hurt can change who you are, as a person by hardening your heart or you can deal with it and continue to love as you've grown too. Sure, your husband hurt you but Lillie, you can't change who you are because of the selfish actions of someone else. You are a wonderful person, wife and mother; don't lose that."

I hug her.

"Let's pray. Dear God, we love you and we thank you for giving us another chance. We thank you for hearing our prayers and for keeping us, all night long. Now God, I come praying for Lillie. Father, I don't have to give you the details, you already know but I need you to deliver. You said you'd be there for her, granting her what she asks, do it. Cover and protect, provide, heal but more than anything; don't allow her to lose the taste for love. God, she's been hurt but you have the power to restore. She's been cast away by man, but you have the power to comfort, cleanse and calm. Keep her heart close to yours and let her feel you, especially the nights she cries. Keep her close to you and don't leave her alone. We thank you and we trust you before you do it. Have your way. Amen."

I wrap my arms around her.

Blair

I keep looking at my watch and my phone. I've been calling Lillie all night and this morning. Leaving out the house, I see her car parked in Ms. Laura's driveway and decide to wait for her to come out.

"Finally," I say rushing over to her. "Lillie, why haven't you been answering my calls?" I ask walking up to her car.

She looks at me and I can tell she's been crying.

"Lillie–"

"Stop saying my name," she yells walking towards me. "You don't have a right to call me anything anymore. Get the hell away from me."

"Look, I know you're upset, and you have every right to be–"

"Gee, thank you for the permission to have feelings. Who knew you'd be so generous."

"I need this loan," I beg.

"And I needed you, but you threw me out like I was nothing. I guess we're even. Goodbye Blair."

"Wait, please. Can we at least work something out? I will sign a contract saying I'll be 100 percent responsible and I'll give you majority share in the new location. Whatever it takes but Lillie, please, I can't do this without you."

"You can't do it without me? Me, the same person you called a nappy headed house wife who lays around all day doing nothing. Me? The one whom you body shame after giving birth to your son? Me, the one you said couldn't survive without you? What can I possibly have that can help you when I don't even have a job? I'm worthless to you, aren't I?"

"You know I didn't mean those things. I'm sorry," I sigh.

"I guess you're also sorry for sleeping with me, lying and pretending to love me and all the things you said. Man," she shakes her head, "you made a complete fool of me, over and over and I let you, but you won't get another chance. These last six or eight months, you've made a mockery of me and this marriage because you knew how bad I wanted this to work. I gave you all of me and all I get is a two-bedroom apartment with the rent paid for two months, clothes and the baby's furniture from the nursery."

"I'm sorry," I repeat.

"Yes, you definitely are but you're also bat shit crazy if you think for a moment, I'm giving you another chance."

"What are you going to do? Huh? We both know you can't survive without me."

"There he is, the real Blair Weaver. Well sir, I'm going to take my life back. Don't come here again," she states.

My face heats up from anger. "You ought to be grateful I even got you a place to live but good luck with surviving because I'm going to have your cards cancelled," I taunt.

"Blair, how do you think she'll survive? She has your son for goodness sakes." Ms. Laura says from behind her.

"Then she should have thought about that before she pulled this little stunt."

"My stunt? Negro please. You're only mad I beat you at your own game. But it's cool. I'll live without you."

"We'll see. After these two months are up, you'll come crawling back to me or be living here with Ms. Laura," I laugh. "Look at you, you're already crying yourself to sleep."

"My tears are temporary but you and I, we're permanently over. You were the one who called last call, didn't you?" she smirks. "Well, consider my tab paid in full."

"Whatever Lillie, you'll be back."

She gets in her car and pulls off. Ms. Laura slams the door.

"Fuck!" I yell.

Making it to Kim's apartment, she's waiting at the door.

"Well?"

"Well what?" I ask. "It's over."

"Damn it, I told you to wait," she says waving her hand.

"How was I supposed to know she didn't go through with signing the papers. You said this would work."

"I didn't count on her not trusting you."

"Well, what now Sherlock? I did everything you told me to do."

She stands up. "We wait. You said she can't make it without you, right? She doesn't have a job and money, she'll be back. Right now, though, I need you to take care of me."

Kim grabs my hand, leading me to her bedroom.

Lillie

It's been a month, but I finally have the utilities in my name and the apartment furnished with the things BJ and I need. Blair called six or more times a day for the first week but after threatening him with a restraining order, he stopped. Now, he only calls every few days with the lie, he's checking on the baby.

Today, I'm at Hazel's restaurant during the beginning of her dinner rush. BJ is asleep in his pack and play in the office. Hazel is short staffed and asked me to work the front until her evening hostess comes in.

Walking up, I see Blair and some chick coming through the door.

"Good evening sir, table for two?"

His eyes widen at the sight of me. "Lillie, you're slumming it already baby? Damn, that didn't take long," he laughs.

"How many in your party, sir?"

"Two," he answers.

"Right this way."

Once they are seated, she looks me up and down.

"Um sweetie, I need a glass of Merlot, chilled to room temperature," she states, "and make sure my glass isn't dirty. He'll take Bourbon, straight."

"Um sweetie, that's what servers are for."

Getting back to the hostess area, Hazel comes over with her hands balled into fists.

"That MFER got some nerve. You say the word and I'll kick him and that skank out."

"No, leave them. I want him to think he's winning at a game he's the only one playing."

Thirty minutes later, I walk into the bathroom then into the stall.

"Girl yes, you should see his wife. She's working here at the restaurant." Laughing. "Baby, I don't see what he saw in that thang because she is not his type at all." More laughing. "Girl, I don't know. He said he put her out and paid for an apartment for two months. Shit, I don't care because I plan on being the next Mrs. Blair Weaver. Then I'll show her how to appreciate all

that chocolate. Yep. Anyway, I got to go. I'll talk to you tomorrow when I get home. Yes bitch, I'm spending the night. Don't wait up."

We flush at the same time. Coming out of the stall, her eyes get big when she sees me. We both wash our hands.

"I'll make sure to take good care of him," she says getting a paper towel.

"You know what they say. Another woman's husband," I pause walking close to her, "can get you beat the hell up. However, no worries sweetie, Blair isn't worth it." I grab the shoulders of her red dress with my wet hands, "but mention my name again in any capacity, trick and you'll see what this thang can do." I run my hands down her arms and then push her out the way.

"Hey, my hostess just got here so you can take off. Thank you for covering. I know I've made you late for Bible study," Hazel says when I walk up front.

When Blair's date walks pass, with the sleeves of her dress wet, Hazel looks at me and we both laugh.

*****

Walking into Mount Carmel Baptist Church, Pastor Saundra Wyatt is up teaching.

"When Job lost all he physically had, he didn't lose his mind. You want to know why? He trusted God. Even after learning his ten children had died; Job tore his robe, shaved his head and fell to the ground and worshipped.

His words are marked on the pages of the Bible, in Job one verses twenty-one and twenty-two. He says, *"Naked I came from my mother's womb, and naked I will return. The LORD gave, and the LORD has taken away. Blessed be the name of the LORD." In all this, Job did not sin or charge God with wrongdoing."*

Sometimes people of God, we'll take a loss. Sometimes, we'll take multiple losses, but will we trust God? Even when Job's body was attacked, and his wife told him to curse God and die, Job responds, *"Should we accept from God only good and not adversity?"*

Sometimes, stuff is going to happen that will cause us to lose. The test will come back positive for cancer and we'll lose our hair and our breasts. The job lays off and we lose pay and possibly our house. Sickness shows up and we might lose momma, daddy or sister. Marriage ends, and you lose the comfortability of spouse. You may miscarry and lose baby.

This doesn't mean you won't feel pain because losing people and stuff hurts. Therefore, suicide is probable, anger is high and mental capacity is diminished after a loss. What do you do?

Acknowledge your pain. Accept that losing can trigger many different and unexpected emotions. Grieve your way, learn the difference between grief and depression and get help. I can't stress this enough. If you know or even think you need help, get it. Stop thinking therapy isn't something we don't, as black people, need. No matter the color of your skin, therapy can help you. Don't be afraid to admit you need help."

She pauses.

"Truthfully, it's after the loss when you'll need help the most. I don't care if it's only to have somebody listen to you cry, babysit or take you out for a meal. Don't drown your sorrows in alcohol or drugs, get help. Surround yourself with somebody who is willing to help you and keep quiet about it. You don't need a person whose lips can't stay closed or those who want to brag because it's you, the person who always seem to have it together, who needs help.

Some of you, in this room have taken losses and it's going to be okay. You'll live and survive it, if you get up. Because think about it. When a home is destroyed by a tornado, fire or storm; usually the foundation stands. Why? Because it's been built to last and hold the house, which means it must be strong and durable enough to bare the weight. When you're in God, your foundation is just as strong and lasting. So, even after the loss, you can rebuild again."

"Wow," I say wiping the tears. I take my notebook and write, I will rebuild again because I'm stronger than I admit. My foundation is solid, and I got this. Lillian Shantay Weaver, you got this.

"Let's pray," Pastor Wyatt says. "Father God, thank you for creating us on a firm foundation. Thank you that even after we've suffered losses, we can rebuild again. Father, for those in the room who are dealing with losses, will you do something for me? Give them strength to acknowledge their pain, give them fresh eyes to be able to see the difference between grief and depression, give them space and time to handle grief and then send them someone who can help.

God, we know loss is tiring, hard, depressing, and can be controlling; but tonight, by your power we shall rebuild again. God, somebody here is angry at self because of the way things have happened but speak tonight so they can forgive themselves.

Release the Holy Spirit in this place to comfort the brokenhearted, to heal the sick, to free the depressed and to turn our ashes into beauty. Don't allow us to sin while dealing with our losses but allow us to be made whole again. We thank you God and it's in your name we pray. Amen.

I know this is a tough subject and for those of you who may need help, text It's Me to 98000 and someone from the church's mental health team will respond. Good night and God bless."

Blair

I walk into the house and it's pitch black. Heading to the alarm panel, I kick something in the floor.

"Shit," I mumble fumbling for the light switch. By the time I get it on, the alarm is blaring. I punch in the code and drop my bag on the floor, next to the shoes that I almost fell over.

My phone vibrates.

"Yeah, no everything is fine. My name is Blair Weaver and the passcode is BJ2. Yes ma'am, thank you."

Going into the kitchen, I turn on the light and stand there.

"What's that smell?" I sniff until I go over to the drawer that holds the garbage cans. "Oh God," I try to keep from throwing up. I quickly snatch the bags out and take them outside. Coming back in, I search through all the cabinets for some air freshener and more garbage bags. Finally finding them and finishing, I shake my head before opening the refrigerator. The only thing staring back is three water bottles, take out containers and spoiled milk.

I slam the door.

Walking to the bedroom, I undress and go into the bathroom to shower. Opening the closet, there aren't any towels. Searching through the dirty clothes hamper, I smell a few before finding one I can use. After my shower, I get dressed in some jeans and a shirt. Good thing, I have clothes clean.

I finish and head out to get something to eat. On the way, I decide to stop by Lillie's apartment. I press the code on the gate and drive in. Parking I walk to her door.

"Who is it?"

"Blair."

She opens the door. "What are you doing here?"

"I wanted to see BJ."

"And you didn't think to call or text, first?" she asks folding her arms.

"Lillie, can I please see my son."

She steps back and allows me to come inside. I stop when I see a dude sitting at the table.

"BJ is asleep. His room is on the left," she states before walking back over to the table and sitting down.

Whatever she'd cooked has my stomach growling. I go into the nursery and look over into the crib. I stand there for a minute until I hear Lillie laugh. Angrily, I shake BJ hard enough to wake him and he starts to cry. I pick him up, he cries harder. After a few minutes of expecting Lillie to come in, she doesn't. I'm bouncing him and he's screaming louder.

"Shh, come on man, quiet down for your dad. Shh. Lillie," I call out. "Lillie."

"What's up?" she asks from the door.

"Can you please take him?"

"No, you shouldn't have woken him up."

"I wasn't trying to. Please," I beg holding the baby out for her to take. She shakes her head. Putting him on her shoulder, she begins to hum while rubbing his back.

"It's okay," she tells him.

After a few minutes, he quiets down and falls back to sleep. She holds him for a few more minutes before laying him down again. I follow her out of the nursery.

"Are you done?" she asks.

"Where is your date?"

Perry comes out of the kitchen drying his hands.

"I told you I'd do that," she smiles at him.

"It was the least I could do after that amazing dinner. Thank you. Mr. Weaver, it's good to see you again." He extends his hand, but I don't take it.

Lillie shakes her head.

"I'm going to get out of your space but call me when you get the shelves to put up."

"Wait, let me get your to-go plate and the basket for Gillian."

When she finally comes back, he kisses her on the cheek and leaves.

"Wow, you're already sleeping with the moving guy who's married. Damn, don't you have standards?"

She rolls her eyes. "You can't be that stupid, oh wait, you are. Get out of my house."

"It's an apartment and I'm paying for it," I correct.

"You paid two months and that's almost up."

"It's still in my name so technically, I don't have to leave if I don't want too."

"Are you really wanting to play these childish games? Better yet, where is Kim or that thot you had at the restaurant? I'm sure one of them can keep you company and out of my business?"

"You are my business."

"Not anymore. Good night," she tells me holding the door open.

"I'll be back and next time, there better not be another man in my house."

She laughs and slams the door in my face.

Getting to the car, I am seething mad. I get my phone and call Kim.

"Hey, what's up?" she answers.

"Did you cook dinner?"

"Cook? Baby, I don't cook but I can order us some takeout. You coming to me or should I come to you?"

"Meet me at the bar."

I hang up and throw the phone into the passenger's seat.

Walking into B Squared, I'm met by Hazel.

"I'm not in the mood."

"What is wrong with you?" she asks following me into my office. "You're not even the same person I've known all these years. Blair, Lillie is your wife."

"Soon to be ex," I correct.

"Do you hear yourself? You and I both know this bar wouldn't have even been opened without Lillie."

"Oh, cry me a river. I made this bar what it is and with or without Lillie, it'll still survive," I holler.

She begins to look behind the door and in drawers.

"What are you doing?" I ask her.

"Looking for the man I used to call brother. The one who had a bold love for his wife and cared for his family because this man, the one in front of me is acting like a bitch."

"You better watch your mouth Hazel. I will not tolerate you calling me out of my name."

"Then man up because you know this isn't right. You threw your wife and son out on the street. For what? What do you have to show for it other than an empty house?"

"A successful bar that's bringing in five figures a month. And who says my house is empty?" I laugh.

She rolls her eyes. "You know you didn't open this bar on your own."

"Will you go, please."

"What would you do if you didn't have this Blair? What would your life be like, if you woke up tomorrow and all God has blessed you with is gone?"

"GO, PLEASE!" I yell.

"Babe, what's going on?" Kim says from the door. "Why are you yelling?"

"Nothing, she was just leaving," I state.

"We aren't done."

"Look Hazel, you've said your peace about something that has nothing to do with you. Now go."

"I pray God has mercy on your rotten, raggedy soul." She stomps out.

"What was that about?"

"Nothing. What did you bring me to eat because I'm starving? Oh, can you do some grocery shopping for my house?"

"Boo, I don't grocery shop. Give me your card and I'll order everything you need."

Lillie

"Hey," Wesley my neighbor says coming into the apartment.

"Hey, come on in," I tell him. "Where's Twyla?"

"She's coming. You know that girl is always slow. Here," he says handing me a bag, "you take the food and I'm going to go look at the sink in your bathroom."

Wesley and Twyla are my neighbors and he is the maintenance man of the complex. Since living here, this past two months and attending some of the functions the apartment throws; I've gotten to know them. Tonight, we're getting together with a few of the other neighbors to play cards.

I take the food he brought into the kitchen. He got wings from Huey's. I take them out of the to-go container and put them on a serving dish, next to the cheese and sausage platter I made.

Before I can finish, there is a knock at the door.

I grab a paper towel to get the sauce from my fingers as I open the door to find Blair standing there.

"What are you doing here again, unannounced?"

"I came to see my son," he says pushing pass me.

"Hold on dude because you don't have the right to barge in. I've told you to call before showing up."

"I don't want to hear all that. Where is my son?" he says beginning to walk towards the nursery. He comes back looking confused. "Lillie, where is BJ?"

"He isn't here. You'd know that had you called."

"Lillie, I–" Wesley stops when he comes out of my room without his shirt. "My bad, I didn't know you had company."

"It's cool Wes, he's leaving."

"Who is this?" Blair questions.

"What's up man, I'm Wesley," he holds out his hand, but Blair doesn't take it.

"Who is this nigga you got in my house around my son," he yells.

"First off, he isn't a nigga, he's African American. Secondly, your son isn't here. Thirdly, I don't have to tell you nothing because you have no right to question who I can and cannot entertain. You severed those ties when you packed my shit."

"Entertain? So, you're a whore now? First it's the Perry dude and now some–"

"Lillie, are you alright?" Twyla asks walking in the door.

"Yes girl, I'm fine. My almost ex-husband Blair was just leaving."

"I'm not going anywhere," he states.

"Either you leave or I'm calling security," Twyla tells him.

"And tell them what? My name is on the lease. If anybody will have to leave, it'll be her."

I laugh.

"Lillie, you want me to get rid of this asshole?" Wesley asks.

"Nah, let him keep on with this little macho man routine. Bible says, resist the enemy and he'll flee."

Twyla and I go into the kitchen to finish getting things set up. I walk into the living room and Blair has made himself comfortable on the couch. I don't acknowledge him. Instead, I grab the remote to my sound bar and turn it on. I search through my iTunes account and play, Ex-Factor by Lauryn Hill.

Dancing, I begin to sing.

"It could all be so simple, but you'd rather make it hard. Loving you is like a battle and we both end up with scars. Tell me, who I have to be to get some reciprocity. No one loves you more than me and no one ever will."

Twyla joins in, "Is this just a silly game that forces you to act this way? Forces you to scream my name then pretend that you can't stay. Tell me, who I have to be to get some reciprocity. No one loves you more than me and no one ever will."

He jumps up and leaves, we laugh.

A few days afterward, while I was out meeting with a divorce attorney and Hazel was babysitting BJ; Blair popped up again and I realize its time I find my own spot. Searching through a box of documents, I realize I left some things in the office at the house. I dial Blair's number, but he doesn't answer. Before I can text, there's a knock on the door.

"This better not be his ass," I mumble.

"Good morning Lillie."

"Hey Perry," I say pulling my robe closed before stepping back to let him in. "How are you?"

"I'm good, can't complain. What about you?"

"Great, actually. How's your wife handling the chemo treatments?" I question.

"So far, it hasn't been as bad this time around, but she wanted me to give you this," he says handing me a card. "It's a thank you for the basket you sent. The ginger really helps with the nausea."

"You're welcome. I've seen how the stress of cancer can burden families and whatever I can do, I will."

"I sure will, and I appreciate you listening to me when I'm here. I don't normally open up about my personal life," he tells me, "but you're a good listener."

"Keeping things bottled up isn't good and I know how hard caring for a loved one is. Whenever you need to talk, I'm here."

He nods. "Thanks, it means a lot. Okay, show me where you want these shelves."

"Actually, I'm not going to put them up."

"Is everything okay?" he asks.

"No, it's time for me to move."

"Is Mr. Weaver still popping up?"

"Yep and he thinks because this place is in his name, he has that right. So, it's time I move."

"I understand that. Well, when you're ready, call and we'll come and move you."

"Thank you and I'll be in touch."

Closing the door, my phone dings.

BJ'S DAD: What's up?

I shake my head.

ME: I need to come by your house to get some papers from the office.

BJ'S DAD: You can stop by whenever you want. I'm not there.

ME: Thanks

After getting BJ up and ready, I head for the house. I park in the driveway and use the front door, even though the garage door is still programmed to my car. Walking in the house, I go to turn the alarm off and notice it is set to stay. I shrug it off and enter the code. Picking up the car seat, I turn to walk to the office when Kim comes around the corner.

"Breaking and entering now," she huffs.

"I can't break into what I own dummy," I say walking pass her.

I go into the office and put BJ down next to the desk. Using my key to open the file cabinet and after a few minutes of searching, I find the documents I need. I'm almost done when the baby starts to cry.

"Hold on sweet pea," I say to him as I finish and relock the cabinet.

"I know, we don't like this place anymore, do we?" I say while removing him from his seat. I sit in the chair to feed him. Getting him latched, I begin to hum and run my fingers through his hair. I lay my head on the back of the chair and close my eyes.

Fifteen minutes later.

"That job must be kicking your ass." Blair laughs.

I open my eyes but don't respond to him. I move BJ and fix my shirt.

Blair is looking at me with a smirk on his face.

"What makes you think a job is wearing me out?"

"You're falling asleep while feeding our son."

"Just because my eyes are closed, it doesn't mean I am asleep. Oh, I see your girlfriend has moved in. Is that why you keep popping up at my place? You can't find peace?"

"Are you jealous?"

"No, actually I'm upset that she's doing such a piss poor job keeping you away from me."

He laughs, "nobody controls me."

I stand up with BJ on my shoulder, asleep; dropping the folder and my keys into the car seat.

"Goodbye Blair."

Blair

"My lawyer says you aren't contesting the divorce," I say when she walks pass me.

"Nope and after the 90-day waiting period, I've asked my lawyer to fast track it. Aren't you excited?" she sarcastically asks.

"Let me guess, you want child and spousal support and part of the bar."

"Then it wouldn't be an uncontested divorce. Dang, does stupid dwell here?"

"Yeah right."

She stops, and I almost bump into her. "If you can't take care of your son without a court order, we don't need it. All I want is to be free from you. You can keep this house and the bar, I want nothing but my sanity. Sooner rather than later."

"Come on, do you think whatever Hazel is paying you will match the lifestyle I've given you? Wake up honey, you will not survive without me."

She keeps walking towards the door.

"Lillian do not walk away from me when I am talking to you," I bark grabbing her arm.

She staggers, the car seat falling from her grip as she almost drops the baby.

"What is wrong with you?" she yells causing the baby to scream. "You almost made me drop our son."

"I'm sorry," I tell her as she clutches him to her chest and I pick up the seat.

"I told you we should get custody of that baby. She's unfit," Kim says walking up.

"Blair, you'd better put a mussel on your puppy."

She laughs. "And if he doesn't, are you going to jump me again? Go ahead, it'll be more evidence when we file for custody."

"Girl, the only thing you'd ever get custody of is that poodle for a wig, you're wearing."

"You can talk about me all you want but we know you can't afford to take care of him. What are you making, $7.25, $8.00 an hour?"

"Whatever I make, it's none of your business. Control your dude and keep him away from my apartment worried about what I'm doing. If you can't, a restraining order will."

"You expect me to believe he still wants you when he has all of this?"

"Please stop fanning your arms," Lillie says to Kim, "the smell is making me sick."

"Kim, stop. She's just trying to ruffle your feathers."

"Feathers," Lillie says, "don't you mean fleas?"

"Keep talking and we'll make sure you never see your son again," I threatened putting my arm around Kim. "As a matter of fact, maybe I'll ask for him in the divorce. I think Kim will make a better mother to my son, anyway."

She laughs. "He isn't property and if you think for one second, I'm scared of your empty threats, think again. You can't even quiet him down when he cries. And the only son of yours she'll ever raise is the puppies she gives birth too. Now, this hasn't been fun, and we shouldn't do this again. You two take care." She says snatching the seat from me and leaving.

I slam the door behind her.

*****

"Blair, do you have a minute," Carson, my head bartender asks.

"Yeah, come in. What's up?"

"When is Lillie coming back?"

"She isn't. Why?"

"Things were different with her. Don't get me wrong, Kim has a knack for increasing the business, but she doesn't know how to work with the employees. We've had two servers to quit today and one yesterday. She's changing the vibe of the bar."

"I'll talk to her."

"Can you do more than that? Look, I've been working with you for the last two years, and I've been running bars for over twelve. This chick is going to run this business into the ground unless things change."

"I'll handle it Carson but thank you for letting me know. Can you call the servers who quit and have them come back?"

"I don't–"

"I promise, they won't have to deal with Kim."

He nods.

"Thanks."

I open my computer and the background, a picture of BJ that I cropped Lillian out of, causes me to pause. I pull up my photos and begin looking through them. I shake my head and pick up my phone.

"What's up?" Kim says walking in.

I lay the phone down.

"I'm glad you're here, we need to talk."

"About?"

"The employees. I've gotten complaints and some of them have even quit."

"Good. There's no way I'm going to have some lazy ass folks who can't respect me running my business."

"Your business?" I question.

"You know what I mean."

"No, I don't. Look Kim, this is my business and your responsibility is not the employees. I've asked Carson to rehire the servers who quit and from now on, he'll manage them."

"Whatever," she says waving her hand.

"I'm serious. I can't have issues with the employees because it's a quick way to ruin business."

"Fine," she stomps out.

"Man, what have I gotten myself into?"

Lillie

Banging on the door.

"I'm coming," I yell before snatching the door open. "May I help you?"

"Are you Lillian Weaver?"

"I am."

"My name is Tawanda Arnett from the Tennessee Department of Children Services."

"Okay, what is this about?"

"May I come in?" she requests.

"Sure," I step back and once she's in, I close the door. "Can I get you something to drink?"

"I'm fine."

She sits, and I go over to check on BJ who is laying on the floor playing with a kick and play toy set I picked up from Target.

"Ms. Arnett, what is this about?" I question.

"Mrs. Weaver, we received an anonymous report that your child, a Blair Weaver, Jr. is being physically abused and you're not fit to care for him. I'm here today as a part of the formal investigation."

"Investigation? You really think I'd hurt my son?"

"Ma'am, I'm not here to judge, only to gather facts and to make sure the minor child is safe."

"I can assure you I'd never hurt him, but I also understand you have a job to do. What do you need from me?"

"Can you tell me about an incident where the child was dropped while in your care?"

"Dropped?" I ask confusingly.

"The report states you may have been intoxicated because you staggered with your son and he fell to the floor."

My leg begins to shake with anger as I catch on to what's happening. "I was at my husband's house, we recently separated, and he was upset about me walking off. I had the baby in my arms when he grabbed me. I staggered but I never dropped my son. Had he fallen, I would have taken him to the hospital immediately. Ms. Arnett, this is only him or his girlfriend being vindictive."

"That may be true, but I still have to investigate such claims. Do you mind if I look around your home?"

"No, feel free."

After a few minutes, she comes back.

"How long have you been staying here?" she asks.

"A little over two months but I'm planning to move soon."

"Why?"

"This place is in my husband's name and he thinks that gives him the right to show up whenever he wants."

"Has there ever been any physical abuse in the marriage?"

"No," I answer. "Emotional yes, but never physical."

She makes some notes.

"Where do you work?"

"I don't. Well, not anymore. I used to be a registered nurse, but I resigned once I had the baby and my husband and I own B Squared bar."

She writes in her notebook before going over to BJ. She sits her things down to get on the floor with him. When she's done, she makes more notes before standing up.

"As part of the investigation, your son will have to be taken to the Shelby County Crime Victims & Rape Crisis Center for the exam by–"

"Rape crisis? You think I'm sexually assaulting my son?" I interrupt.

"No ma'am, this is where the exam will take place by a specially trained nurse practitioner. I've set an appointment for you on tomorrow at 9 AM. Here's the address. You may also be interviewed again so prepare to be there a few hours. Thank you for your time and I'll be in touch."

Once she leaves, I get my phone and call Blair. He doesn't answer so I continue to call him back to back. He still doesn't answer. I grab BJ, my purse and keys and head to the place I know he'd be.

Pulling up at the bar, I get the baby from his car seat and go straight for his office.

"You low down dirty bastard," I fume bursting through his office door.

"Lillie, what is your problem?"

"It's one thing to not give a damn about me but I never thought you'd intentionally try to hurt our son."

"Can you all excuse us," he says to the four people in his office.

He closes the door behind them.

"Lillie, I don't know what you're talking about."

I'm crying and walking in circles. "I got a visit from Child Protective Services about a report of me abusing our son. Now, he has to be taken to a rape crisis center in the morning to be examined. You know I'd never hurt him. I only staggered because you grabbed my arm."

"Lillie, whatever you got going on or have gotten yourself into, it's not because of me," he says going back to his desk.

"Are you serious? This lady specifically asks about me dropping our son and it just so happens to come after leaving your house, the other day. Now, you want to play dumb like you don't know what I'm talking about?"

"It seems to me, if you don't have anything to hide, do the examination. Now I have to finish the meeting you rudely interrupted."

"You cowardly, egotistical bastard. After everything I've done for you, this is how you treat me? I'm still your wife and the mother of your son and you'd risk me losing him? Why? Huh? We both know you can't physically take care of him because he doesn't know you. How many times has he laid on your chest to feel your heartbeat or your skin? How many times have you put him to sleep? How many times have you looked into his eyes or spoke, so he can know your voice? How many times have you fed him?"

"What does that matter? He doesn't have to know me to raise him," he shrugs. "If it comes out, you're unfit to raise my son, I'll hire a nanny."

"As much as I'd like to wish evil on your soul, it's probably already black. Instead, I pray God never gives you the vengeance you fully deserve. The pain and disgust I feel for you, in this moment, is nothing compared to what God is witnessing. I'll be vindicated of what I've been wrongly accused of because the righteous live by faith but the wicked are doomed, for they will get exactly what they deserve."

"Yeah, yeah. Can you go now?"

*****

Sunday morning, I walk into Mount Carmel needing my soul revived. On Friday morning, I spent four hours dealing with questions and BJ being medically examined and prodded. After everything was over, Ms. Arnett states she'll be in touch with either a resolution or continuation of the case but couldn't say when.

I sign BJ in at the church's daycare before heading into the sanctuary. The choir is up singing, I told the storm by Greg O'Quinn.

"I told the storm, to pass, storm you can't last. Go, I command you to move today. Storm, when God speaks, storm; you have to cease that's what I told the storm. No weapons formed against me shall prosper, I don't have to worry about a thing. I'm a conqueror through Jesus Christ and He's going to bring me out. Oh yes, He is. It's amazing grace that's brought me safe thus far and grace is going to lead me home. I stood on solid ground and told my storm and you need to tell your storm today. Winds stop blowing, floods stop flowing, lightening stop flashing, breakers stop dashing, darkness go away, clouds move away; that's what I told the storm."

Pastor Wyatt

"How many of you are in a storm today? Well, if you tell the storm to go, it must go because Bible says, I can say to the mountain, may you be lifted up and thrown into the sea, and it'll happen. But I must really believe it will happen and have no doubt in my heart. Anybody here ready to tell your mountain of mistakes, offenses, unbelief, naysayers, trouble, anger, inflicted pain by others and neglect; be ye removed from me? Anybody ready to tell the storm to go?

Anybody ready to look at the giant that's been taunting you and telling it to flee, knowing if you believe and do not doubt, it can be done? Anybody else, this morning, sick and tired of being thrown by the winds of your storm? Anybody, today, fed up with looking at your mountain? Then declare with me, I don't have to fight it, but I will speak against it? Yeah, say it loud and proud. I don't have to fight it, but I will speak against it."

"I don't have to fight it, but I will speak against it," the congregation repeats.

"I know this is the time I should be taking a text and I may or may not. But somebody needs to tell your enemy; no boo, I'm not about to get my hands dirty, I'm going to use my words. Tell him, her or them; you can play all the games you want too, I'm not about to stoop to your level but I will use my words.

Nah, I'm not about to go back and forth with you, I'm going to use my words. I'm not getting out of character, I'm using my words. For my God tells me in Luke seventeen and six, *"if you had faith like a mustard seed, you would say to this mulberry tree, 'Be uprooted and be planted in the sea'; and it would obey you."*

Believers of God, without faith our words are just words but with faith, our words become power. Without faith, we must fight in the flesh but with faith, we sit back and allow the word to do the work. Without faith, I can speak to the tree and it'll waive back but with faith, I can speak to the tree and it'll move. Without faith, you might hurt my feelings but with faith, you can talk all day and night and I don't care.

No longer will I remain quiet, I'm using my voice. No longer will I let you upset me, I'm using my voice. You can't intimidate me anymore, I'm using my voice. Your threats, they don't scare me any longer, I'm using my voice. And when I use my voice coupled with faith, you've got to flee. I ain't scared no more, I got faith and I'm using my voice. I won't be quiet, this time because when I shut up, the enemy rises up.

When I hush, you take that as an opening to hurt me. When I close my mouth, you think you've won. If I keep quiet, I might not survive. If I keep quiet, you might keep taking advantage of me. I can't be quiet because I'm sick of you and your mess, and it's time you get the hell on. I won't be quiet, instead I'm going to get my faith up and yell louder."

People are crying out all over the sanctuary.

"People of God stop doubting the ability that's placed on the inside of you. Remove doubt of if it can happen when Bible says, it will. Get rid of doubt and believe. Some of you have been fighting your mountain for far too long and some of you are just getting started; stop holding back. This doesn't mean you curse folk out, but you correct them. Tell them, no boo, that worked with the old me, but she's gone now, and this is what we about to do. All you need is faith, the size of a mustard seed and a voice.

God bless you Mount Carmel. Oh, I feel some chains breaking. Yeah, they meant it for evil, but God meant it for your good. Good afternoon Mount Carmel may the Lord bless you real good. Glory! The devil tried but he won't win. Hallelujah God. No matter what you've been threatened with, have faith and do not doubt. Whatever the battle you're facing, have faith and do not doubt.

I don't know who I'm talking too but don't ever lose your voice again, men and women of God. Yeah, it may hurt, it may not make sense and it may look like you won't win but have faith and do not doubt. The obstacle may be bigger, things might look impossible, but have faith and do not doubt."

I pause while the musicians play music.

"The doors of the church are open."

The choir stands and begins to sing, *the storm is over now*, by Kirk Franklin.

Lillie

I open the door to let Hazel in.

"Hey boo," she says, "I bought dinner."

"Thanks, but I'm not hungry right now."

"I'll put it in the kitchen. BJ asleep?" she asks walking back in the living room. "Lillie, hey, are you okay?"

"No."

"What is it? Did you hear from CPS?"

I shake my head no. "It's just the weight of everything."

She comes over and holds out her hands. "Come," she beckons, "let me wrap my arms around you."

"I'm good."

"No, you're not and right now you need to know you aren't alone. Lillie, you're always being strong and you needing somebody else to lean on doesn't make you weak. What you're going through is hard and its heavy but I'm here, lean on me."

I stand, and she pulls me into her.

"I just don't understand–" I stop and push away from her.

"Lillie?"

"What kind of perfume is that you're wearing?"

"Um, it's called Daisy by Marc Jacobs. Why?"

"Where did you get it from?" I ask.

"A friend. Lillie, what's going on?"

I move farther away.

"A friend, huh? What friend?"

She doesn't say anything. "Are you and Blair having an affair?"

"Hell no," she screeches. "Lillie, this is me. Do you really think I'd sleep with your husband?"

"You may not be sleeping with him but are you having sex with him?"

"No," she yells. "Where is this coming from?"

"That perfume, I remember him coming home smelling like it because it stinks."

Her mouth is open, but she doesn't say anything.

"Tell me the truth," I say above a whisper.

"I'm not having an affair with Blair. Maybe he came to the restaurant and I hugged him, but I promise, we're not having an affair."

"Stop lying," I scream, "that funky ass perfume was all in his shirt."

"Lillie, I'm not lying. Please, you can call him, and he'll tell you."

"Get out of my house," I order.

"No, I'm not leaving with you thinking I'm having an affair with your husband. Lillie, you're my best friend. You've been there for me when I didn't know how to be there for myself. You've helped me and there's no way I'd betray you. You have to believe me."

"I don't have to do shit. Get out."

"No," she states. "I'm going to call Blair."

She picks up her phone and calls him, putting it on speaker.

"What?" he answers.

"Did you tell Lillie we're having an affair?"

He laughs.

"Blair, you have to tell her it's not true," she says beginning to cry. "Tell her we're not having an affair. I would never sleep with you."

"I wouldn't call what we've done sleeping, Hazel baby."

"Oh my God," she hollers, "please don't do this Blair. Tell Lillie the truth."

"We can talk about it tonight when I see you. Love you," he says and hangs up.

"Blair," she yells. "Blair. Lillie, he's lying. Please," she begs grabbing my arm. "I wouldn't do that to you."

I snatch away from her. "Get out of my house and I never want to see you again."

"Lillie, he's lying," she's repeating while I walk into my bedroom and slam the door.

Sliding down to the floor, on my knees, I scream. "Lord, I'm tired of being the bigger person and turning the other cheek. I'm always helping and being what everybody needs but who's there for me? Where is the person I can lean on? Huh?" I begin hitting the floor as my screams become sobs. "Why is everyone turning against me? Lord, please help me."

Feeling someone touch me, I jump. It's Hazel. I look at her before bending over, wrapping my arms around myself. She begins walking around, crying and calling out to God.

"God, your word says in my distress I can call on you and from your temple you'd hear my voice and come swiftly on the wings of the wind. Well God, it's not me tonight but my sister Lillie. God, she's crying out to you, hear her and show up. She needs you to calm and comfort, remove her from the traps of the enemy and avenge her name. God, only you know why we must suffer, be lied on and misused but you said you'd never leave us. Show up now for my sister, her son and her sanity.

God, allow her to feel you, especially during moments like this. Father, it's your word that says, you'll rescue us from the strong enemy, those who hate us for they are too mighty for us. Please do it. You don't have to give us details, just deliver. And God, we know that sometimes we must suffer but will you give strength. We know we must go through, but will you walk with us because my sister Lillie, she needs you. Wrap your arms around her that she'll survive this storm, she'll come out of this man-made fire unburned and with her mind. Give her sight to see the right things, ears to hear what needs to be heard and a mind to handle them all. Thank you, Father and amen."

She sits beside me, pulling me into her.

"You can be angry at me, for now but I'm not leaving you and neither did I betray you. I love you Lillie," she tells me.

*****

A few days later, I'm leaving a meeting with a realtor when my phone rings.

"Hello, this is she. Yes," I listen as Ms. Arnett gives me the findings of the investigation. "Thank you. No, I appreciate you doing your job. Thank you for calling. May God bless you too."

Ms. Arnett said the case has been closed because they could find no evidence of abuse or my inability to care for BJ. They will have to submit the findings, to both of our attorneys since we're going through a divorce, but they shouldn't reflect against me. I do a happy dance on the way to the car.

Blair

I walk into Hazel's restaurant.

"Good afternoon is it just you for dinner?" the hostess asks.

"No, I need to see Hazel Russell."

"One moment."

She walks to the back and a few minutes later, she motions for me. I follow her to Hazel's office.

"Blair, what the hell are you doing here? After the stunt you pulled the other night, you got some nerves."

I laugh. "Well, if you get your friend to help me, I'll admit I lied."

"I'm not helping you with nothing, you smug bastard."

"You will because you value your friendship with Lillie. So, here's what I need you to do. Call her, send her an email, hell it can be a smoke signal but tell her she needs to cosign my loan."

She laughs.

"Look, I'm desperate and I can't do this without her. The bank is willing to give us the loan but without her I can't get the full amount I need."

"And you think I'd convince her to help you after you kicked her and your son out on the street. You flaunt your flings in front of her like the last ten or eleven years have meant nothing. Blair, I saw how hard Lillie worked on your dream–"

"Yada, yada; I don't need a lesson in character and damn sure not marriage from someone who's never been married."

"Dude get out of my office. I can't help you. I'd rather lose my friendship with Lillie than to see her get entangled with you on anything else. You don't deserve her or her name."

This time I laugh. "Are you sure?" I ask taking a seat.

"Very."

"The seed of doubt has already been implanted in Lillie's brain about us and with a little embellishment on my part, she'll never speak to you again."

"She might not but you also won't have a loan. So, take you and your embellished," she puts in air quotes, "ego and get on."

I stand up and plant my hands on her desk. She jumps back.

"I'm tired of playing nice. Either you tell Lillie to sign the loan or I'll make your life hell. All it'll take is a call from the health department to close this little place down because I'm sure they'll find some mice or something in the kitchen. Now, you have two days."

"And you can go to hell because I have cameras."

I drop my hand from the door knob and slowly turn around.

"See, it's Negroes like you that make women like me install cameras because some of you lie more than women. Well, you'll never be able to say Hazel did anything unprofessional behind closed doors. So, you can start this game but baby I promise you won't like how it turns out. Close the door behind you and have a bless day."

I get to my truck and I'm pissed. I hit the steering wheel, over and over before starting it and pulling off.

A car horn sound.

I'm dazed for a second then I throw the truck in park, turn it off and unfasten my seat belt.

"Man, you didn't even look before you pulled out in front of me. Are you okay?" a gentleman asks walking up to me.

"Yeah, I'm fine. Are you?"

"I'm good. My wife is calling the police, do you need an ambulance?"

I shake my head no while stepping back to look at the side of my truck.

"Great, just freaking great."

*****

Eight weeks later, I'm standing in the courtroom listening to the judge read off the terms of my divorce from Lillie. We had to wait 90 days before the judge would even think about hearing the case. It's called a cooling off period to see if things can be reconciled.

Because neither of us contested the divorce and were able to work out a custody agreement, our attorneys were able to get us on the docket before the holidays.

I've been stealing glances at Lillie, but she won't even look in my direction. The last time I heard from her was when I needed help with the insurance information for my truck. She refused and has since removed herself from the policy. She won't even talk to me concerning BJ, my visits are handled at Ms. Laura's.

My lawyer nudges me.

"Mr. Weaver are you with us?" the judge asks.

"Yes sir, I apologize your honor."

"Were you a resident of Tennessee for six months, immediately before you filed for divorce?"

"Yes," I state.

"I've looked over the Marital Dissolution Agreement and Mrs. Weaver, it doesn't seem as though the assets of the marriage have been divided fairly and equitably; are you sure this is what you want?"

"Yes sir, your honor. I only need what I asked for, he can keep everything else."

He looks at me.

"Very well. Mr. Weaver, are you in agreement with the custody plan that has been put into place that states you are to split all cost, for minor child, with the custodial parent, Mrs. Lillian Weaver?"

"Yes sir."

"And you've worked out an amicable visitation schedule that you've both agreed on, right?" the judge questions.

"Yes sir."

"You will each carry your own medical insurance and cover your own

court costs and attorney fees, is that correct?"

"Your honor," I interrupt. "I'd like to cover the court cost and attorney fees for Lil—I mean, Mrs. Weaver."

"Is that okay with you, Mrs. Weaver?"

She nods.

"Very well, the agreement will be amended. Mr. Weaver, you're asking the court to grant you a divorce on the ground of irreconcilable differences?"

"Yes, your honor."

"Very well. According to the Marital Dissolution Agreement, before me, both of you have agreed to the following. There will be no spousal support paid by either of you–"

He begins to read the agreement and I look over at Lillie.

My attorney nudges me again.

"Is that correct?" he asks us.

"That's correct," I say.

"That's correct," Lillie adds.

"Then it is therefore ordered by this court, divorce granted."

After shaking my lawyer's hand, I rush out to catch Lillie.

"Lillie," I call out.

"What's up Blair?"

"I'm sorry."

She smiles. "What are you sorry for exactly? Could it be for kicking me and your son out, having affairs, lying about having an affair with my best friend, trying to forge my name on a loan, the child abuse case filed against me or for the blatant disrespect you've shown me over the last year? Which is it just so I'm clear?"

"All of it. I made a mess of things and I can only hope–"

"Nah, don't do that. Don't act like you're concerned about me. It's been over six months and you've had ample time to apologize, not that I need it because I'm over it but still. As for whatever it is, you're hoping for, spare me because I don't trust you or your hope anymore. Happy Anniversary, by the way."

Lillie

"Girl, this is amazing," I shout to Hazel over the music. "Thank you for doing this."

"It's not every day, you get divorced from a jerk so, here's to a new beginning and almost New Year."

We clink our glasses together and down the shot of Patron. A song comes on and Hazel drags me to the floor. After five songs, I'm sweating, out of breath and in need of some water.

"Baby, it's been too long since I've danced," I tell her.

"Me too but hey, it's great cardio."

"Let's get out of here because I'm starving."

"We can always hit up CK's like we used to do in college."

"Yes," I sing. "I haven't been there in forever."

Thirty minutes later, Hazel and I are enjoying our food.

"So, what are you going to do now that you're divorced and on your own?" she asks me.

"I'm going back to work at the West Clinic. It's only part time but I'm excited."

"Really? Why? I know you don't need the money."

"I know but I've been helping Perry–"

"Wait," she interrupts. "Perry is the moving company guy whose wife was your patient before?"

I nod. "Her name is Gillian and she's going through chemo for the second time in 18 months. I've been over to their house a few times helping her after the treatments and I miss it. Not the nastiness of it but the part about caring for the patients."

"You've always been great at that. I remember when your grandmother was sick, you took very good care of her."

"I know, and God knows I miss them. If my grandpa was still living, I probably would have moved back to Mississippi and reopened the diner."

"Not that dingy ass diner Blair is always bad mouthing?" she laughs.

"Child forget him. That diner saved his tail, plenty of times after his mom ran off with the money he'd saved for college. Anyway, with BJ turning a year old soon, I think it's time I do something for me."

"Well, I think it's a great idea and I'll help with BJ."

"Hazel, thank you." She is trying to swallow her coffee to stop me from saying it. "No, listen. I never got to thank you for that night at the apartment. I had a feeling Blair was lying but, I was mad and hurt. It seemed like everything was hitting me at once. Man, it felt like my heart was in a vice grip," I say patting my chest. "Yet, you stayed. Not only that, you prayed and held me into the early morning. Thank you for being there because I needed you."

Her eyes fill with tears as she grabs my hand.

"Lillie, you're my best friend. If I can't be there for you while you're hurting or willing to petition God, while you're in the middle of a storm, what good is our friendship? God knows, you've been there for me. When I wanted to end my life, you were there," she shakes her head and wipes the falling tears. "I'm just grateful evil didn't tear us apart because you know I'd never do anything like that to you, right?"

"I know," I blow out a breath to calm my emotions and use the napkin to wipe my face. "Okay, enough of this mushy stuff. Tell me what's been going on with you. We've only been ta!king about me the last six months and I need a change."

"Well," she drags out, "you remember the friend who gave me the perfume?"

"The stanky perfume?" I laugh, and she throws a slice of toast at me.

"It's not heifer but yes, him. It's Charlie," she says hiding her face behind a napkin, "my Sous Chef."

I pretend to choke.

"Lillie are you okay?" she jumps up.

"Yes wanch," I slap her hand, "why didn't you tell me."

"Girl, I thought you were choking."

"Whatever. I knew something was going on with you two. I knew it. Why didn't you tell me and how long?"

"We've been official for almost four months and I don't know. I guess I wanted to make sure it was real. I've been through too many relationships and I'm tired of giving myself to folk who can easily hurt me. Lillie, I want to be loved, for real."

"Um hello, you're preaching to the choir. My divorce, from the man I've been with over eleven years, was final on our seventh wedding anniversary. Imagine thinking you're going to grow old with someone who can pack your shit and evict you from the marital home, with your baby, without even a care." I pause.

"Hazel, that man hurt me in parts I didn't even know existed. Down in crevices I never knew pain could seep, it did, and it hurt badly. It's the type of pain nothing can ease. Girl, there were nights I wanted to scream until glass broke or cry myself to sleep but I couldn't because I didn't want BJ to feel the stress. Shoot, I've purchased so many new plates due to me breaking them in anger," I take a deep breath. "I wasted so much time. Then he had the nerve to want to apologize at the courthouse. Nah boo, keep that empty apology because I don't need it."

"Don't you though?"

"What?" I ask after sipping my orange juice.

"You may not need it, but don't you deserve an apology?" she enquires.

"No, what I deserved was him being honest with me. I deserved respect. I deserved his love and loyalty. His apology means nothing because I no longer trust his character. Bible says love rejoices at the truth."

"Will you try love again?"

"One day, I will because love didn't break my heart, Blair did. Anyway, tell me about Charlie."

"Lillie, he's amazing," she begins.

Before we realize it, we've sat in CK's over three hours. By the time we leave, the sun is coming up. I make it home, to a place that's all mine. I closed on it the day after the divorce was final. I haven't moved my things from the apartment yet but it's mine. I turn off the alarm and reset it. Dropping my purse on the kitchen's island, I begin walking through the house.

"Lord, I'm grateful to you for keeping your promise to me. You said you'd turn my mourning into dancing, and you've did just that. Thank you for never taking your hands from me. Thank you for not allowing my heart to turn to stone. Thank you for not allowing another moment of my time to be wasted. You kept my mind and I've seen you work, this last year, like never before. Negative words from a man who vowed to love me, they didn't break me. Disrespect, it didn't delay me. Pain, it pushed me, and I owe it all to you.

God, I may not know the plans you have for me but I'm ready. Guide me, so that I'm not outside your will. Give me strength to forgive with my heart and my words. Cover and protect me and my son. This home, I give to you to use as you see fit. Protect it on every side, from the beginning of the driveway to the farthest point of the property line. Don't allow evilness to congregate here and lack to ever find me.

Grant my son the chance to grow up here, within the walls of a home filled with sounds of joy, peace and laughter. Allow us to make memories to past down to other generations. God, I know I'm not perfect, forgive me. I know I've made mistakes and will probably make more, forgive me. I may not always say the right thing but forgive me. Forgive and restore me so that I'm who you've called me to be. Then God, if returning to work is part of your plan, open the door. If you make the way, I'll follow. Amen."

I continue to walk around the empty house until tiredness overtakes me. I lock up and head back to the apartment, for the final time.

Blair

Time has been moving and a lot of things have changed. Lillie and I are divorced and although I thought I'd be happy, I'm not. The holidays didn't make it any better, fact is, I've started drinking more. I haven't been spending a lot of time with BJ, like I promised, out of selfishness and stupidity.

I'm sitting in my office at the bar nursing a glass of Bourbon, after everyone is gone home. Business is great, and we even celebrated our third anniversary tonight and yet I feel like something is missing. I keep running my finger over the B Squared logo on the glass before swallowing the rest of the liquid, laying my head back on the couch and closing my eyes.

"Are you crying?" I ask Lillie when I stop sweeping to look at her.

"Yes," she says, "but I can't help it. Look at this," she holds the glass up with the logo. "This is our baby. We own a bar, babe. Can you believe this is our reality?"

I go over to her and wrap my arms around her.

"Nah, it's crazy to think this was all a dream I used to draw on paper," I kiss her on the neck, "and now it's here."

"Listen to you sounding like Tupac," she laughs. "But I feel you because this place was packed tonight, and the reviews have been amazing. Pretty soon, we'll be making a profit to hire some help and then I can stop washing dishes."

"And I can stop sweeping floors," I add.

"Man babe, when we first started praying for this, I knew God would answer but to stand here seeing the tangible display of His blessing; I'm in awe," she says.

"Just wait until next year when we're celebrating one year but for the third year, we're going to throw the biggest party ever."

"Why the third year?" she inquires.

"Because three represents perfection and we will be. I'm going to wear a black tuxedo and you'll have on a black dress, that goes all the way to the floor with a pair of red bottoms."

"Red bottoms?"

"Yes girl, it has to be epic. By then, you'll no longer be working because this place is going to blow our wildest expectations. You'll see."

She turns to face me.

"I appreciate you dreaming and I'm here for all of it, but I'm not quitting my job. Hear me out," she says covering my mouth to keep me from speaking. "This is your dream and I've been more than happy to help you but being a nurse is mine. If I quit, I may lose my identity."

"Babe, you'll never lose your identity because you can always be my nurse," I say kissing her neck.

"I'm serious B. I want us to both enjoy our dreams and we can do that as long as we stay together."

"Okay," I relent, "but if you change your mind, just know I'll support you the same as you've supported me."

She wraps her arms around my neck.

"Deal," she kisses me.

My phone vibrates, pulling me from my thoughts. I answer and press the speaker button.

"Baby, where are you?" Kim whines. "I've been waiting on you for over an hour."

"At the bar."

"Why?"

"Because I needed some time alone."

She sighs. "You're not in your feelings, are you? Look Blair, we celebrated three years of B Squared being in business tonight, you're grossing over six figures a year and things will only get better once the second location is open. Now, lock up and come home."

"We didn't celebrate anything Kim, I did."

"Oh," she chuckles, "you are in your feelings."

"Things haven't gone as I planned, that's all."

"When one plan falls through, you create a new one. Babe, we're–"

"You keep saying we," I snap. "There is no we."

"Of course, there's a we. Negro, I'm the one helping you get contracts with distributors–"

"Because that's your job and you're paid well for it. Everything else is a bonus. You know what, I can't do this."

"Me either, this whining is nerve wracking. Come home and let me relieve that stress. I'll keep on the heels."

"No, I can't do this relationship anymore. You're fired."

"Fired? Boy bye. You can't fire me, I made you."

"Made me? Kim, you've been around for less than a year and whether you know this or not, I was made before you showed up. You may have added to me but that's what your job description says. Besides, the only thing you made me do," I pause for emphasis, "was ejaculate."

"Wow," she drags out.

"I'm sorry but I never should have started a physical relationship with you because it has blurred the lines of business. Ever since you came into my life, it's been chaotic to say the least."

"Business? Sweetie, this stopped being business months ago when I stepped up and started doing wifely duties."

"Okay," I chuckle, "either I'm drunk or you're delusional because you aren't my wife and nothing you've done constitutes that."

"Thank God," she exclaims. "Your wife could never compare to me. Nonetheless, if you think I'm about to bow out gracefully, like the one you threw away, think again. You owe me for all the times I've had to listen to you whine, pick up the slack at the bar and handle your sexual desires. You promised me I'd be the next Blair Weaver and that's exactly what you're going to give me. All those trips you planned, things you vowed and this house, yep, I'm getting everything."

"That's where you're wrong. After what you did to my son, I can never trust you again. You could have gotten him taken away from his mother."

"Like you care," she scoffs. "If you cared about your son or his mother, you would have stayed at home instead of spending time with your head between my legs. Everything I've done has been with your permission, whether you voiced them or not. You want to play victim but no, boo, you're the one calling the shots. Your marriage is over and the lack of a relationship with your son is because of you, not me. Now, come home."

"You know, you finally said something right. This is my fault."

"Great, we're getting somewhere. It's your fault, things didn't go according to plan etc. Are you coming home now?"

"Yes," I reply.

"Good."

"But I need you gone. The business and personal relationship between us is over. I'll have the accountant cut you a check for the remainder of your contract and it'll be mailed to your apartment."

"Nothing is over until I say it is and if you think I'll fade into the night like your precious cargo, I mean wife, think again."

I hang up the phone.

Kim begins calling back to back. I turn the phone off and stretch out on the couch. I wait a few hours before heading to Lillie's apartment. Turning my phone on, Kim has filled my voicemail and sent 67 texts. I ignore them to call Lillie, but she doesn't answer.

Knocking on the door, there's still no answer.

"Lillie," I yell knocking harder. "Lillie, please open the door."

A door opens but it's her neighbor.

"Dude, it's like seven in the morning," he says.

"I know but I need to speak to my wife."

"Well, you won't be doing it today because she isn't there. She moved a few weeks ago," he smirks.

"Moved? Moved where?"

"If she didn't tell you, neither am I." He closes the door.

"Damn it."

I keep calling Lillie's phone but now it's going straight to voicemail.

"Ms. Laura will know," I say rushing to my car.

Before I pull off, I get a feeling in the pit of my stomach, so I head back to the bar to have the locks and alarm code changed. Sitting in my office, I call Carson to give him a heads up and my accountant to have her cancel the business card Kim has.

An hour later, the men are almost done changing the locks while I'm on the phone with my lawyer to assist me in composing an email to my list of distributors.

"Good morning, as distributors and/or contract holders with B Squared Corporation in Memphis, TN; I wanted to make you aware of a recent change. Kimberly Prather is no longer affiliated with our company, as of today. All business with her ceases. If there's anything you need with any new or outstanding contracts, please contact Carson Roman or James Morgan. Both of their contact information is below. If you have any questions or concerns, please contact me directly. I look forward to continuing with business as usual.

Cheers,

Blair Weaver, owner and operator."

"Yes," James, my attorney says. "That covers it. CC me and we'll go from there."

"Thanks James."

"Blair be careful. I've seen women like Kim and they don't go away easily. I'll start the paperwork for a restraining order, just in case you need it."

I finish everything at the bar and head home to lay down for a few hours. Pulling up, I gasp when I see the word liar spray painted on the garage.

"What the f–" I mumble pressing the garage door opener and throwing the truck in park. Running into the house, the kitchen is filled with smoke and the detector is blaring. I push the door open and leave the garage up while going over to turn off the stove. I snatch the pot from the eye and throw it into the sink, turning the cold water on.

Getting a chair, I remove the smoke detector and its batteries. Turning the corner in the living room, my mouth falls open. It's demolished. The TV is smashed in, all the pictures broken, and liar is spray painted on the wall.

"You've got to be kidding."

I walk down the hall and stop at the door of the bedroom. Same thing.

"Fuck," I yell, dialing 9-1-1.

"Yes ma'am, I need police to 1222 Field Chase Rd. Yes, my house has been vandalized. Yes, I know who did it. Her name is Kimberly Prather."

Lillie

I'm in the car, headed to Ms. Laura's house when I turn up the radio.

"Okay ma'am, you want to put your boyfriend on the jackass wall. What did he do?" the radio announcer asks the caller.

"He dumped me."

"Okay and?"

"He doesn't get to dump me," she angrily states. "I've been waiting on him to divorce his wife for almost a year and now he thinks he's going to dump me. Hell no."

"Oh, so he's married?"

"Yes, well he was. His divorce was final a few weeks ago."

"And then he dumped you? Girl, move on," the female announcer says.

"No, I'm not moving on. He owes me."

"Owes you what exactly?"

"His last name," she sighs. "Y'all don't understand. He and his wife hired me to help grow their business but two months in, him and I started sleeping together."

"Wait," I say turning the volume up more. "Is that Kim?"

"Did the wife know?" the male host asks.

"She found out–"

"And I beat your ass, tell them that," I yell to the radio.

"His business just turned three years old and now, when we should be celebrating, he thinks he can fire me."

"He fired you, not dumped you?"

"What's the difference?" Kim asks angrily.

"It means he never considered y'all to be in a relationship. See, when you're in a relationship, you get dumped. When you're doing business, you get fired. Chick, consider this a loss, hope for a nice severance package and referral."

"No, no, no;" she begins to yell. "I was his woman, handling his needs, picking up dinner, ordering groceries for his house, giving him head whenever he asks for it–"

"Whoa," the hosts are laughing, "that's too much information."

"He gave me the garage and alarm code, to his house and everything. Now, he thinks he can just push me to the side. Well, he's wrong."

"Okay, but I don't understand why you're choosing to blast him on the radio. This isn't going to make him want you. Come to think of it, he may hate you."

"I don't care," she yells. "I've been loyal to him and he's going to do what he said. He promised I was going to be his wife. He doesn't get to go back on that. I will not stand by and let him treat me like he did his ex. He may have thrown her out like garbage but I'm not going away peacefully."

"Lady, you were a piece of ass who handled his business. Cut your ties sister."

"I'm going to cut something, but it won't be ties."

"Hello, ma'am you there. Hello. Wow, that chick is crazy. Listen, if you're a man in Memphis, TN who just got divorced and celebrated three years in business; you may want to watch out," the male host states.

"And men, y'all must stop playing with these women's feelings. You can't make promises, break them and expect the woman to play nice. This chick is hurt and pain like that can cause people to do some crazy things. My brother, whomever you are, you better be praying."

Pulling into Ms. Laura's, I see the police at Blair's house. He watches as I drive pass to park. Getting out, I shake my head and continue to the door.

"What's going on with Blair?" she inquires after opening the door.

"I'm guessing Kim, but that's his problem. How are you?"

"Child, I have no complaints. BJ is up watching baby boss or boss baby, whichever it is, in the living room."

Before I can sit down, Hazel calls.

"Hey–wait, what?" I laugh. "Where? Whose page? No girl, I'll have to look. But did you hear her on the radio? A mess. Okay, I'm about to and I'll call you back."

"What happened?" Ms. Laura asks.

"Kim called 107 FM this morning to blast Blair because apparently he fired her and she's mad. Now, Hazel says she's making posts on the B Squared Business page on Facebook."

I log into the bar's account and shake my head.

"Oh my God, this girl has posted pictures of her and Blair having sex," I tell Ms. Laura. My mouth hangs as I continue to scroll.

"Nothing worse than a woman scorn."

"Well, I don't feel sympathy for either of them," I tell her. "They got exactly what they bargained for. He was willing to throw away his family for this. Serves him right."

"Are you going to go over and talk to him?"

"No ma'am, there's nothing more we can discuss. He set these events in motion and it'll be him who must stop them. Anyway, I finally got everything put up at the house."

"Are you excited?"

"I am, and I can't wait for you to see it."

"I'm so happy for you Lillie. Speaking of happy, how was your first day back at the West Clinic," she asks yawning.

"It was amazing. I didn't realize how much I missed being a nurse, but I'll share all the details with you later. BJ and I are going to get out of here and let you rest. Thank you for keeping him, last night, and I know you won't allow me to pay you, but I have something for you." I hand her an envelope.

"What is it?"

"Open it."

"Lillie," she tears up, "what did you do?"

"When we first moved to this neighborhood, you became a mother to me. You opened your home and invited me in, you taught me how to cook certain dishes and you helped me be a better wife and woman. I didn't have that growing up because my mother died in child birth and my grandmother when I was fifteen." I pause to wipe the tears. "Giving birth to BJ, you've become his grandmother, helping me raise him and you never ask for anything in return.

This is just a small token to say thank you and I love you."

"You, you," she stutters, "you paid off my house?"

"It's the least I can do."

She comes over and wraps her arms around me.

"Thank you for loving me," I tell her.

Later that night, after getting BJ settled in his crib, at home, I walk into the kitchen for a glass of wine.

The doorbell rings. I scrunch my face because I'm not expecting anyone. I stop in my tracks when I get to the front door.

Blair

"Blair, what are you doing here and how did you know where I lived?"

"I have my ways. You haven't been answering my calls."

"I don't have to answer your calls unless it's your weekend with BJ. Funny thing is, you don't call then. Oh, but your son is doing well, and he enjoyed his first birthday, that you missed."

"I'll make it up to him."

"We won't hold our breath. Now, what's up?"

"Whose house is this and how much is the rent on this place? Man, this is nice."

"I wouldn't know."

"What do you mean? You don't know how much you're paying to live here?" I laugh. "Don't tell me your sugar daddy that owns the moving company is paying your rent. Damn. Well, I shouldn't be surprised because your stuff is good enough to make a man put out."

"You're drunk, and you need to leave before you get your ass kicked."

"Why are you so hostile? I asked a simple question that you're having a hard time answering. If you're whoring yourself out to pay the rent, what's the rate because I could use some of you."

Before I can continue, she punches me in the mouth.

"Ah," I yell then laugh. "Feisty, I like it." I try to push my way in again.

"Blair, I'm not playing. Leave my house before I call the police."

She pushes me away and slams the door in my face. I stand there for a minute before stumbling back to my car.

*****

"Dude get up. They've been calling for you the last hour."

I open my eyes and when they focus, I jump up. "Where am I?"

"Jail," somebody screams, "now shut up."

"Weaver, get your ass up and let's go."

I walk to the cell door, confused and funky. The deputy jailer grabs my arm, dragging me down a hall.

"Your bail has been posted, sign here."

He pushes the pen into my hands then a large envelope. Another jailer pushes me through another door.

"Blair, man you look horrible," James says to me.

"How did I get here?"

"Hell, you don't remember?" he asks.

"I don't remember anything."

"You were arrested three days ago and charged with drunk driving, resisting arrest, having an open container and speeding. You spent the weekend in jail."

I press my back against the wall.

"Blair, you've got to get your shit together or you risk losing everything you worked for. These last few weeks you've been spiraling."

"What's the point? Kim has ruined me with all the crap she put on Facebook. Then my house. You should see my house."

"And? You aren't the first person to be exposed and you won't be the last. Hell, man up brother because this is the price you pay when you play games."

"I'm not playing games."

"Yes, you are. You knew exactly what you were getting with Kim, yet you still ignored the warning signs. Man, you kicked your wife out and divorced her like she was nothing, for a piece of temporary ass."

"James, I get it but I'm not in the mood for a lecture."

"You should be, and I should have been a better lawyer."

"This isn't your fault."

"I know it's not," he says. "That's not what I meant. I should have been better in calling you out on your mess, before you got here. Blair, look at where you are because of your actions. You're a grown man who needs to grow the hell up and take responsibility for the fire you started. You can either put it out or allow it to continue to destroy everything you've worked for."

Tears begin to fall.

"I know you've been going through a lot but come on Blair, this isn't you. You didn't even spend the holidays with your son, you missed his first birthday and now with a DUI, you can lose your liquor license and your business. Is that what you want?"

I shake my head no.

"Then get yourself together. Carson has been handling the bar and I've spoken to all the distributors and they've agreed to keeping their contracts. I filed the paperwork for a restraining order on Kim but this personal shit, this is on you to fix. Take some time off and clear your head because you have court in two weeks. For now, go home, take a shower and fix your life. Here," he drops my keys in my hand, "I got your car from impound and I'm charging you for every dollar I've spent."

Getting home, the house is still torn up from when Kim vandalized it. I walk pass the mess, like I've done for the last weeks and into my bedroom. Undressed, I step in the shower.

Flashes of the last time Lillie and I were in here began to play.

"When did I stop mattering to you?"

"You haven't. Everything that has happened is because of me, not you."

"But it doesn't stop the pain coursing through me each time my heart beats. You're the only man I've loved this way and I used to feel like nothing else mattered because your love made me feel ten feet tall. Now, I feel like I'm not worth the dirt on your shoes. Just go Blair. Please."

I slide into the floor of the shower and begin to sob.

"Lord, I'm sorry," I cry. "I've made a mess of things and it's typical to call on you now, but I need you. Please forgive me."

A few days later, the garage door and the walls of the house have been repainted. I had to hire a cleaning company and purchase another bed and mattress because Kim cut the old one up, along with most of my clothes.

I decided to take a few weeks off from the bar, to do like James says, and get myself together. That starts with where I am tonight. I've been sitting in my car, for over twenty minutes, my fingers gripping the steering wheel and my stomach is in knots.

Turning off the truck, I get out. Walking inside the doors of Mount Carmel, I feel like I'm in a foreign land.

"Blair?"

"Deacon White, how are you?"

"I'm good son. How are you? It's been a while since we've seen you."

"I know but I'm good," I tell him.

"Well it's great to have you back. Go on in, Pastor just got up to teach."

Pastor Wyatt

"Did you know the tongue; this small muscular organ is the reason we taste and articulate sound? Do you know without the tongue; a person would be capable of forming sounds yet no longer able to form words? Maybe you did but are you aware the Bible says in James three and six, *"And the tongue is a flame of fire. It is a whole world of wickedness, corrupting your entire body. It can set your whole life on fire, for it is set on fire by hell itself."*

Verse seven and eight says, "*people can tame all kinds of animals, birds, reptiles, and fish but no one can tame the tongue. It is restless and evil, full of deadly poison."* Is that interesting to anybody else or just me because I find it strange that God would give us control over something so powerful? Then I realize, God gives us authority because it's up to us on how we use it, the choices we make and the things we speak.

Therefore, you must be careful when you speak things, when you put your mouth on folk and I don't mean physically but with your words. With the tongue, you can corrupt your entire body and set your whole life on fire. That's what Bible says, not Pastor Wyatt. Then you'll have the audacity to get mad at God when the stuff you put in motion starts to gain traction. You'll find yourself angry at the world when things, you gave power, begins to take control of your life.

When you keep saying, I hate it here, you'll never find peace where you are. When you say, folk get on my nerves or they make me sick; your brain starts to believe what it keeps hearing. My back is killing me or it's too hard are things we're accustomed to saying. But people of God, if our tongue is a flame of fire and the words, we speak come off our tongue, they aren't burning but they are cooking.

Listen, when you put a pot on the stove and turn the fire on, whatever is inside the pot cooks, right? The aroma of what's cooking goes into your nostril and signals to your brain that you're hungry. When you're hungry, you do what, eat what's in the pot. Sometimes though, you aren't hungry, but the smell alone will still make you eat.

When we speak, our words are cooking on the fire of our tongue and the aroma is reaching the signals in your brain. You must be careful what you speak. Shoot, there's only so many times you can keep telling somebody you don't love them before they believe it and leave. You can't keep telling folk you don't need them and expect them to show up when you do. You can't keep cutting folks with your words and then complaining when they bleed all over you.

My sisters and brothers, when you realize the weight of your words, you'll stop saying just anything. I don't care if you're joking, your words carry weight and you ain't even got to lift a finger. Your words can set your entire life on fire and you can sit right where you are. Don't believe me?"

I pull my phone from my back pocket and lay it on the podium.

"Your words have power and you don't have to lift a finger," I say again. "Hey Siri," I call out.

My phone dings and after a second, Siri's voice says, "I'm listening."

"Can you find the phone number to Mount Carmel Church?"

"One possibility I see is Mount Carmel Church on Rasler Road in Memphis. Do you want that one?" Siri asks.

"Yes."

"The phone number for Mount Carmel Church on Rasler Road is plus one, 9017865545. Would you like to call it?"

"Yes," I reply.

I turn the phone around for them to see then press to end the call. "Speaking can set stuff in motion you never intended to move. Your words have power but here's two words that can help you make right what you've wronged, I apologize or forgive me. Some of you allow your words to do like my grandma says, write a check your butt can't cash and now, you're left somewhere by yourself looking foolish. Learn to shut up. I'm sorry, maybe I should say, hush but no because some of y'all need the harshness. Shut up, you talk too much. Who used to sing the song, you talk too much?"

"Run DMC," somebody says.

"Yes," I reply grabbing my phone and pulling up the lyrics. "Song says, you're the instigator, the orator of the town. You're the worst when you converse, just a big mouth clown. You talk when you're awake, I heard you talk when you sleep. Has anyone ever told you, talk is cheap? You talk too much, you never shut up." I laugh when others join in to sing.

"Proverbs ten and nineteen tells us, "*too much talk leads to sin*. Be sensible and keep your mouth shut. And pray, asking God to clean your heart because when there's residue, it'll come out in your words. Going back to the pot, if you don't clean it properly from the last time you used it, you run the risk of it tainting whatever else you put inside the pot. If you get nothing else out of tonight, know that your words have weight, your tongue is fire and what you speak can manifest. Pray, clean your heart and guard your tongue. Let us pray."

I wait until everybody stands.

"Dear God, I come tonight in submission, petitioning your throne. God, thank you for allowing us to come to you and for another chance to study your word. Now God, forgive us. Forgive us for not realizing the power of our words. God, we've hurt and cut down people with our tongue. We've ended relationships, you ordained with our tongue. We've pushed away those we were supposed to love and help, with our tongue.

God, we're sorry. We're sorry for taking advantage of the power you've given us. Where we should be speaking life, we've spoken death. When we should have been speaking anointing, we've spoken anger. We're sorry God. Clean our tongue and our hearts so that we no longer destroy what you've given us to speak life into. Clean our tongue and our heart so we stop burning bridges you've designed us to travel over. Clean our tongue and our hearts so that we no longer sever what wasn't meant to be.

Clean us up, God, so we can speak life and not death. Clean us up because we've made a mess of things. No longer will we speak without thinking and no more will we allow negative and hopeless words to control or damage our life. We now know the weight of our words and the strength of our tongue. Thank you, God, and amen."

Lillie

I roll my eyes when I see Blair's car pull into my driveway. I get BJ out of his car seat. With my hand on the opener, Blair steps forward.

"Lillie, I'm not here to cause trouble. Can we please talk?"

I don't say anything.

"Please," he states.

"I'm going against my better judgment but fine."

I wait until he comes in before letting the garage down. Inside, I stand BJ on the floor.

"Oh my God, he's walking?" Blair exclaims.

"He's been walking for two months."

"Man, I've made a mess of things," he says squatting in front of BJ who stumbles over to him and when Blair grabs him, he laughs. Blair bursts into tears.

"I'm so sorry," he keeps saying to BJ. "I missed your birthday and everything."

BJ begins to squirm. He lets him go.

"Man," he sighs.

I give him time to get himself together.

"You good?"

"Yeah," he sniffs. "I'm sorry."

I ignore his theatrics. "Can you keep BJ company while I warm his dinner?"

"Sure."

I watch him take BJ's hand, leading him to the living room.

I pull the roast, potatoes and green beans from the refrigerator. While the pots are warming, I mix together ingredients for hot water cornbread. Thirty minutes later, I go to get them and stop when I see BJ climbing over Blair. They're both laughing.

Rolling on his back, Blair sees me. I smile before calling for BJ. Getting ready to walk off, I invite him to eat with us.

"The plates are in the cabinet and the silverware is in that drawer," I tell him. "Fixing plates is the treatment husbands get."

I wipe BJ's hands before putting him in his high chair and grabbing both of our plates. Sitting beside him, he holds out his hand for me to take.

"Thank you," I tell him before saying grace. "Amen."

I look up at Blair who's staring.

"He knows what it means to say grace?" he asks shocked by BJ's gesture.

"Children mimic the behavior they see and it's our custom to say grace before we eat."

"It's just–I missed out on so much."

"You keep saying that but he's young and doesn't have to know you used to be an asshole."

"I was talking about with you too," he clarifies.

"Yeah, well that ship has sailed and sunk."

We eat in silence. Blair goes back for seconds. When we're done, I put the dishes in the sink.

"You can put your plate on the counter. I'll get it once I'm done giving him his bath."

"Can I do it?" he asks.

"Do what?"

"Give him his bath," he clarifies.

"I, uh–"

"I can give him a bath, Lillie."

"It's not you I'm worried about but come on."

He follows me into BJ's bathroom. "Here, you can undress him while I run the water."

I get his towel, pamper, pajamas and body oil out. I explain what to do. "He's all yours but–"

"I got this," Blair interrupts.

I put up my hands and leave out, stopping to change into some leggings and tank top. Coming from the kitchen, once I'm done cleaning, Blair is standing there, and he's soaked. I laugh.

"I was trying to warn you that he likes to splash the water, but you said you had it. Did you have any trouble putting him down?" I ask while getting him a towel.

"No."

"Give me your shirt and I'll dry it."

Turning around, after putting his shirt in the dryer, I gaze at his chest.

"Lillie, I'm so sorry for everything," he says walking closer to me. "I miss you."

For a moment, the words get caught in my throat.

"I miss my family," he whispers in my ear, his hand barely touching my neck.

A moan slips out.

"Give me permission to make love to you," he says against my lips.

For a second, I pause but then I allow him to kiss me. He quickly removes my leggings and I don't stop him. Unfastening his pants, he enters me, and I cry out.

By the time the dryer signals, we're done. My feet touch the floor and I take a moment to steady my breathing. Reaching into the dryer, I give him his shirt.

"Let yourself out," I tell him before walking out.

"Wait," he says bumping into the wall, trying to pull up his pants, "that's it?"

"Were you expecting a cigarette and night cap?"

"No," he says, "but maybe some conversation."

"Look Blair, you're the only man I've been with in over eleven years. You were here, I needed an orgasm and you gave it to me. That's it. Please leave out the front door because it automatically locks."

I stop by the nursery and look in on BJ before going into my bathroom to shower. Thirty minutes later, the sight of Blair sitting on my bed scares me.

"What are you doing?"

"Lillie, please talk to me."

I let out a deep breath. "What is there to talk about?"

"I need you," he states, and I laugh.

"You need me?" I repeat. "This must be a joke." I tighten my robe and lead him back to the front of the house.

"It's not and I didn't come here for sex, I came to get my family back."

"Do you hear yourself? Negro, it's too late to get your family back. Where were you when I needed you? Those nights I longed to be laid under my husband, but he didn't come home or the times I'd had a rough day with a colicky baby and you never offered to help? I've raised our son, alone his entire first year of life and now you need me. Hell no.

You don't get to come here and disrupt what I have going, only to leave me broken again. Not anymore.

You didn't want me, you discarded me like trash and now you need me. Well motherfucker, I needed you and instead, you gave me a two-bedroom apartment. Showing up at Bible study, one night, isn't going to change you or my perception of you. You showed me who you are, and I believe it."

"Lillie," he says grabbing my hand, "please forgive me."

"I have forgiven you but there'll never be another us. You hurt me, Blair and you broke your promise. I asked you not to allow the success of the bar to go to your head, you did. I asked if you'd still love me if I gained weight or my hair turned gray and you said you would, but you didn't. In its place, you used your words to cut to the very essence of my soul.

The place that used to house love for you, you removed, bit by bit, each time your mouth belittled me. Yet, I stayed because I thought this was a phase you were going through and each night, you made me dislike you more and more. After everything," I say, tears choking my words, "after everything I gave you."

"You're right. I took you for granted by allowing what I've accomplished to change me."

"It's not just about you," I yell. "You're so freaking selfish. You didn't accomplish this on your own yet it's always I and not us. You didn't get here by yourself."

He sighs. "I don't know what to say that won't upset you."

"Say the truth. Regardless if it makes me mad, be honest. It's all I've ever asked of you. If you knew you no longer wanted to be married, you should have said that. Yet, you took my love and exploited it as a weakness and now, because you showed up at church, I'm supposed to believe you've changed."

"It was never you, Lillie. I took my eyes off the road and by the time I reopened them, I'd crashed. I thought I was going in the right direction, never realizing, I was no longer in my lane."

"Great analogy, where did you get it from Iyanla Vanzant?" I mock.

"No, I realized it, after waking up in jail with a DUI."

Blair

"Kimmy drove you to drink, huh? Well, it serves you right."

I look at her and she shrugs.

"Doesn't feel good to have no one in your corner, does it? Welcome to my world because this is how you made me feel every freaking day. And for what, a few more zeroes in the bank account? Blair, it took two years for you to become a person I didn't even recognize. Two years," she restates. "But you know what pisses me off the most? Watching you celebrate what we created with someone else. Kim wasn't there, at the beginning when we had to wash the dishes at the bar, ourselves. She wasn't there when we had to go to every bank, in the city, before one took a chance on us. She wasn't there when we almost lost our home trying to keep the lease on that building. She wasn't there yet she got the dress and the shoes."

My mouth opens to reply but no words come out.

"Yeah, I saw the pictures of her in the long black dress and the red bottoms. Everything you promised me, she got. I can give her credit for one thing though. She was right when she said, you are a liar."

"Lillie, as always, you're right. I messed up but what else can I say? I'm sorry," I yell.

"Heard, loud and clear. Good night."

"Why can't you give me another chance? I know I'm the reason we're divorced, I cheated and chose money over you but I'm sorry and I've learned my lesson. You said you'd forgiven me, didn't you?"

"I have, for our son's sake but that doesn't mean I'll give you access to me."

"What do you mean? We just had sex, without a condom. You did give me access to you."

"I gave you permission to enter my body, not my heart and I'll get a plan B in the morning. Look, I'm tired and I have to work tomorrow but this is your weekend to get BJ, are you picking him up or not?"

"You're working again?"

"Yes," she sighs heavily.

"Why, is it to pay for this house because I can help you?" I tell her. "I know the rent must be expensive."

"It's not about the house and I don't need your money. I'm working because if you've forgotten, nursing is my passion. Always has been."

"I know but I thought you wanted to be home and raise BJ."

"I did and I am."

"But you're working again."

"You don't get it, do you? I stopped working to do what I've always done, help you build your dream. I love nursing and I put it on the back burner for you."

"Why do you keep saying that? This was a mutual agreement we made. I didn't make you quit."

"You didn't have too. Blair, think for a moment. How would it have been possible for me to stay in the field of nursing with a baby, while you spent 16 to 18 hours at a bar? How could you travel to different distilleries and take meetings all times of day, if I were still working? How could I look over contracts and manage the money, if I didn't quit?"

I don't say anything.

"You never stopped to see things for what they truly were. You were able to be the success you needed, in the front because I was handling the back. I wasn't spending money on clothes and shoes, I was tithing to God's house, from the money being made. I wasn't up all night arguing with you, I was up praying over our family and the bar. I held up my end of my vows, you didn't but you were quick to call me lazy and good for nothing."

"I know Lillie and there's no excuse for my behavior. Babe, every minute I regret ever taking you for granted. Even at the bar, the employees miss you and that's due to me. I love you. Can't we go to counseling or something?"

"No, you can go, I'm good. I've seen all I need to see and heard what I need to hear. You don't respect me and going to counseling isn't going to fix that."

"It will, if you try."

"If I try? I wasn't the one who caused this," she sighs. "Please go."

"I am but I'm going to keep trying until I get you back," I state moving close to her.

"Please don't."

"And I'm going to cut you a check to help with your rent. How much is it?"

"For the last time, I don't need your help."

"Stop being proud and allow me to help you. I know you've been helping Hazel out at the restaurant, and now you're back working. Let me help you. Think of it as child support for BJ."

"Put it into an account for him."

"Lillie–"

"Blair, I don't need your money," she yells. "I don't need your money because there is no rent. This house, it's mine, my name is on the deed and there is no payment."

"How? I don't understand. Where'd you get the money?"

"Do you remember when my grandfather died, two years ago, and I begged you to go with me to take care of his affairs and you wouldn't? I guess that dingy café and raggedy house in Mississippi was worth more than you thought. You'd know but you never had time to talk to me. The loan you tried to get, I could have given you the money, but you were too busy closing my tab, after calling last call."

Her words daze me.

"Blair, it was never about money for me. All I wanted was you. The bar was your dream, it's what you always talked about and I put myself second to make sure you got it. I was the reason B Squared was able to make it because truthfully, we should have closed the first year. I sacrificed me, and you never knew it."

"Why? Why didn't you tell me?"

"Would it have mattered? Sure, you probably would have treated me differently, had you known what I was worth, but it wouldn't have been genuine because you equate dollar signs to success. Dude, money isn't what makes you successful, it's your reputation and righteousness that does."

"Wow, I," my words travel off. "Why didn't you take half of the bar, in the divorce?"

"I don't need or want it besides, the accounting firm we hired to handle the bar's expenses, it's mine and, I'm also part owner of Hazel's restaurant."

"You're lying," I start to laugh. "Whew, you almost had me for a second. You own an accounting firm, yeah right."

"I have no reason to lie to you," she calmly states. "I've actually invested in a few profitable businesses over the last year."

I stand straight up. "I don't believe it."

"Suit yourself."

"Prove it," I state.

"I don't have to. Whether you believe me or not, that's your problem."

"How did my lawyer miss this?"

She smiles. "When we paid the loan off for B Squared, I removed my name from the business and that allowed us to get an agreed or uncontested divorce. Due to this and because of us agreeing to everything, we provided all the information. It's not my fault your lawyer didn't question my finances. Besides, you were the one who told him I had no income, remember." She smiles and hunches her shoulders. "Should have waited before declaring that last call, huh? Goodnight Blair."

Two Months Later

Lillie

I have music playing and my glass filled with my favorite wine. BJ and I are dancing in the living room when the doorbell rings.

I leave him there while I run to open it for Blair.

"Hey," he stops and backs up. "Wow, you look amazing."

"Thank you. Come on in, BJ is ready."

I can feel his eyes burning a hole in my back. "I didn't pack much because I know he has clothes at your house," I tell him before handing him the bag.

In the last three months, Blair has gotten better with his relationship with BJ. This is the first time he's spending the night, at his house, and I'm taking full advantage by going out.

Blair still hasn't said anything.

"If you have any problems or questions, call me," I continue. "Blair, are you listening?"

"No," he chuckles. "I'm sorry. You're distracting me."

"Oh, well focus. Here's his bag. It has his cup and his pacifier because he sometimes needs it to sleep. Don't forget to oil his skin after his bath or he'll have you up most of the night. Um, I think that's it. Any questions?"

"Nope," he says.

"Well okay." I pick up BJ, give him a hug and kiss, handing him to Blair.

"Do you have a date or something?" he finally inquires.

"Yep."

Coming out of the kitchen, the doorbell rings again.

"Damn," the voice on the other side of the door says. "Girl, you look amazing."

"Thank you," I blush. "Come in."

"James," Blair states, "what are you doing here?"

"I'm here for the lady of the house," he answers, eyeing me.

"You're dating my lawyer?" he asks me.

"No boo, I'm dating James," I correct.

"How long has this been going on? Have the two of you been seeing each other all this time?"

"Blair, bring your tone down before you scare BJ and because I really don't owe you an explanation. However, for the sake of keeping things cordial with us," I exhale, "I'll answer you. James and I ran into each other, about a month ago when I went to meet with my lawyer and we started talking. This has nothing to do with you, B Squared or legal matters. We're two adults enjoying each other's company."

"Is this why you moved my services to another attorney in your firm?" he asks James.

"Yes, I didn't want there to be a conflict of interest."

"Then why not tell me?"

"Truthfully, I didn't have too," James replies looking back at me. "Blair, we're all adults and I didn't need your permission to build a friendship with Lillie. She's a great woman, resilient, God fearing and a wonderful mother. She smells great, knows how to take care of a house and a man, works, faithful to her church, pays her tithes, has her own identity and she's someone I can build with. She's gorgeous and that thing she does, when she bites her lip, drives me crazy. Oh, she loves music and I enjoy her company. I hope this isn't going to be a problem," he smirks, sliding his hands into his pocket and I begin to fan myself.

"Friendship, huh? Is that all this is?" Blair questions.

"Not if I can help it," I answer moving next to James. "Blair, you can choose to have a problem with this, I hope you don't, but it won't matter either way. Regardless of what happens between James and I, it has nothing to do with you. We're finally in a better space, can be in the same room and even co-parenting. Don't allow this to change things."

He slowly walks over to James and extends his hand. BJ reaches out his fist for James to dap. We all laugh.

"Treat her better than I did, or you'll have hell to pay," he tells James.

"I plan too."

Blair grabs BJ's bag and when the door closes, James pulls me into his arms and we start to dance.

"Are you ready to go, Mrs. Weaver."

"Not yet, I like being right here with you."

"Well, I promise–"

I place my finger over his lips. "Please don't make me a promise, they can be broken but show me by your actions."

"I can do that," he responds kissing me.

Blair

I open the door to Kim.

"What are you doing here?" I look at my watch. "It's after ten."

"Can I come in?" she asks.

"Hell no."

"I didn't come to cause any problems, I want to apologize."

"Say it from there."

"Blair, please."

"My son is asleep, please don't wake him." I step back to let her in.

"Oh, you're babysitting now?" she asks sounding disgusted.

"No, I have my son for the weekend. Kim, say what it is you need too and leave," I tell her.

She sighs. "Dang, you don't have to be so nasty."

I move to reopen the door.

"I'm sorry," she blurts. "Blair, I know I should have said this months ago, but I was scared. I acted totally out of character when I destroyed your home, blasted you on social media and the radio," she continues rattling off stuff she did, "but I was hurt."

"That still didn't give you the right. Yes, I admit my part in all of this because I never should have led you on to think we would be together. That's the only reason I didn't file charges on you, but you took things too far."

"I know, and in the moment, I wasn't thinking. I only wanted you to feel like I was, angry. You were throwing me away, like I was nothing after all that time together, making promises and then, just like that, you called it quits."

"Yet, you laughed at Lillie, knowing I was treating her the same way. Isn't it crazy how we'll do to people what we don't want done to us?"

"You're right but she was your wife, not mine."

"True and I'm paying for those mistakes every day," I admit. "If I could turn back the hands of time."

"You'd still make the same mistakes," she states. "It's part of the path we must take and regretting it now, doesn't change things. Anyway, I'm sorry and thank you for not pressing charges," she says smiling and playing with her purse. "I kept checking the warrant website to see if I was going to be arrested. It's been stressful to say the least."

I nod.

"Blair, can we try again?" she asks.

"Try what again?"

"Us, the relationship," she states.

"Kim, we can't. I realized, although it was too late, we're toxic together. After everything happened, I started drinking more, then I got arrested for a DUI. Thank God it didn't cost me my liquor license, but I did get hit with a huge fine and probation for a year. Listen, I'm not blaming you, but I've made a lot of mistakes, this past year and I just don't see how us getting together will produce anything good."

"We can try," she whines grabbing me. "I love you Blair."

"No, you don't. You loved what I promised you. Kim, look at how I treated Lillie."

"I wish you would stop saying her name," she huffs. "I'm not her and I'd never allow you to treat me like that."

"No, you'd allow me to treat you worse if it means red bottoms and fancy vacations. No offense, but you aren't ready to be anybody's wife."

"What is that supposed to mean?" she questions folding her arms.

"You don't cook, clean or know how to grocery shop. I also have a son—"

"And? All those things can be rectified by paying someone."

I laugh. "Not everything is about money and some things can't be bought. That's something I've had to learn. I wish you the best of luck, but you and I would never work, long term."

"What about a friend with benefit arrangement?" she smirks.

"Don't you want more than that?"

"Eventually, but for now, I'll take what I can get."

"I'm sorry Kim. If I've learned anything, it's that I'll never treat another woman the way I treated Lillie. It wasn't fair to her and it wouldn't be to you, either. I can only thank God she's forgiven me because I surely didn't deserve it."

"Are y'all back together or something?"

"No, we're co-parenting and it feels great," I correct her.

"Listen to you sounding, uh, so unBlairlike," she frowns. "Where is the man I fell in love with?" she asks moving closer and rubbing her hands on my chest. "He'd have this dress torn off me and my legs in the air by now."

I grab her hands and hold them in front of me. "He's gone. The person you see, is the real Blair Weaver. The one you met, was a very bad representation and I don't ever want to see him again and neither should you. You're beautiful and smart, stop settling for anything and learn your worth. Don't ever allow another man to treat you like I did. You deserve better."

She's staring at me.

"Are you okay?" I inquire.

She snatches her hands away. "I don't like this Blair. Call me when you get out of this funk and you're ready for me and the things I can offer."

"Don't wait around for that call, sweetie."

She rolls her eyes and storms out.

I close the door behind her before going back to the nursery to check on BJ. Standing at his crib, I look at the picture of him, Lillie, and I that's hanging in his room. Lord knows, I regret making the last call on our relationship, but it has opened my eyes.

I almost lost everything, thinking I knew the real meaning of success and relationships. Walking into my bedroom, I pick up the notebook laying on the nightstand, reading over the scriptures from last week's Bible Study.

James, chapter four, verses four through ten.

You adulterers! Don't you realize that friendship with the world makes you an enemy of God? I say it again: If you want to be a friend of the world, you make yourself an enemy of God. Do you think the Scriptures have no meaning? They say that God is passionate that the spirit he has placed within us should be faithful to him. And he gives grace generously. As the Scriptures say, "God opposes the proud but gives grace to the humble."

So humble yourselves before God. Resist the devil, and he will flee from you. Come close to God, and God will come close to you. Wash your hands, you sinners; purify your hearts, for your loyalty is divided between God and the world. Let there be tears for what you have done. Let there be sorrow and deep grief. Let there be sadness instead of laughter, and gloom instead of joy. Humble yourselves before the Lord, and he will lift you up in honor.

"Man," I shake my head. "I ignored all the warnings that were trying to prevent my fall and I messed up God's plan for my life with two words, last call."

I lay the book down and fall back on the bed.

Thank you all so much for reading Last Call. I hope you enjoyed it as with every release, I pray something shared has helped you. Whether it be a song, a scripture or even words written; I pray you've felt God through the pages.

Although this book is fiction, if by chance, it has triggered unresolved emotions for you, I pray that your faith doesn't fail. If you're in the need of prayer, you can email me at authorlakisha@gmail.com. However, even with prayer, if you're in need of counseling, don't hesitate to get because therapy isn't a bad thing.

Until next time, keep reading.

Lakisha

About the Author

Lakisha Johnson is a girl after God's own heart, boldly handling one part of her purpose ... the writing.

Lakisha has been writing since 2012 as has penned more than seventeen novels, devotionals and journals. You can find topics of faith, abuse, marriage, love, loss, grief, losing hope etc. on the pages of her many books. Thanks to the most amazing readers, her latest series, When the Vows Break and Shattered have ranked among Amazon's top 100 in the African American Christian Fiction Genre.

In addition to being a self-published author, she's also a wife of 21 years, mother of 2, Co-Pastor of Macedonia MB Church in Hollywood, MS; Sr. Business Analyst with FedEx, Devotional Blogger, the product of a large family from Memphis, TN. and more. She's a college graduate with 2 Associate Degrees in IT and a Bachelor of Science in Bible.

Lakisha writes from her heart, as she hopes the messages, on the pages, will relate to every reader. Therefore, she doesn't take the credit for what God does because if you were to strip away everything; you'd see that Lakisha is simply a woman who boldly, unapologetically and gladly loves and works for God.

Ask her and she'll tell you, "It's not just writing, it's ministry."

Again, I thank you for taking the time to read my work! I cannot express what it means to me every time you support me! If this is your first time reading my work, please check out the many other books available by visiting my Amazon Page.

For upcoming contests and give-a-ways, I invite you to like my Facebook page, Author Lakisha, follow my blog

https://authorlakishajohnson.com/ or join my reading group Twins Write 2.

Or you can connect with me on Social Media.

Twitter: _kishajohnson | Instagram: kishajohnson | Snapchat: Authorlakisha

www.kishasdailydevotional.com

Email: authorlakisha@gmail.com

Also available

Covet

Karis (pronounced Car-ris) and Darius Toney has been married for seven years. Their marriage isn't perfect, but they've made it work. They're active members of True Vine MB Church, she's a photographer and he own a tire shop. Things are, well, they are good.

Until the day, their life becomes the object of somebody's obsession. The only downside, they don't know who it is. This person, in the darkness has a yearning, a desire to possess something Karis and Darius has ... they just didn't know it yet.

https://www.amazon.com/dp/B0865W6GBC

When the Vows Break

Dearly beloved, that's how it begins, what God has joined together, let no man put asunder; that's how it ends. Happily married, wedded bliss and with these rings, we do take; but what happens to happily ever after when the vows break?

Secrets, lying, cheating, drugs, alcohol and temptations prove that not everything is what it seems.

Will the chaos of it all be more than they can take? Find out in part 1 of the series … When the Vows Break

https://www.amazon.com/dp/B07V7139BW

Shattered

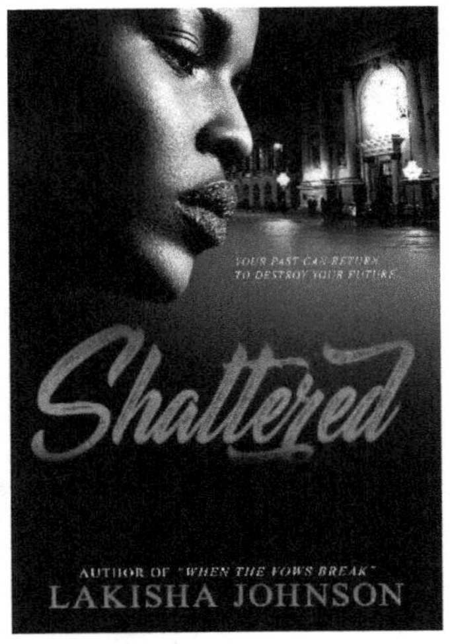

Shattered, a word that means broken into pieces or exhausted and it sums up Camille's life, perfectly.

You met her in When the Vows Break and if you remember, Camille Shannon is who she is. Unapologetically Cam with no holds barred and want what she wants. Until eighteen months ago, when she came face to face with a demon of her past and it sent her spiraling.

From unfaithfulness to drugs, to love and loss; she's experienced it. Some of it is due to her actions yet when she tries to get her life together, it's proving to be harder than she expected.

Broken

Gwendolyn was 13 when her dad shattered her heart, leaving her broken. Her mother told her, a daddy can break a girl's heart before any man has a chance and she was right. Through many failed relationships and giving herself to any man who showed interest, she knew she had to get herself together. So, she gave up on men.

Until Jacque. He came into her life with promises to love, honor and cherish her; forsaking all others until death do they part. Twelve years later, he has made good on his promises until he didn't.

https://www.amazon.com/dp/B07QZCW9ZX

The Family that Lies:

Forsaken by Grayce, Saved by Merci

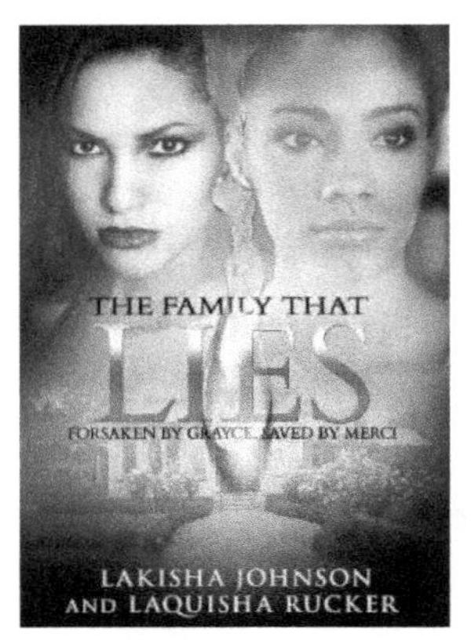

Born only months apart, Merci and Grayce Alexander were as close as sisters could get. With a father who thought the world of them, life was good. Until one day everything changed.

While Grayce got love and attention, Merci got all the hell, forcing her to leave home. She never looks back, putting the past behind her until … her sister shows up over a decade later begging for help, bringing all the forgotten past with her.

Merci realizes, she's been a part of something much bigger than she'd ever imagined. Yea, every family has their secrets, hidden truths and ties but Merci had no idea she'd been born into the family that lies.

https://www.amazon.com/dp/B01MAZD49X

The Family that Lies:

Merci Restored

In The Family that Lies: Merci Restored, we revisit the Alexanders to see how life has treated them. Three years ago, Merci realized she'd been a part of something much bigger than she ever could have imagined. Sure, every family has their secrets, hidden truths and ties but Merci had no idea she'd been born into the family that lies ... without caring who it hurts!

Now, years later, Merci finds herself in the midst of grief, a new baby and marriage while still learning how to pick up the broken pieces of her life.

https://www.amazon.com/dp/B07P6LGQQ6

The Pastor's Admin

DISCLAIMER This is Christian FICTION which includes some sex scenes and language. ***

Daphne 'Dee' Gary used to love being an admin … until Joseph Thornton. She has been his administrative assistant for ten years and each year, she has to decide whether it will be his secrets or her sanity. And the choice is beginning to take a toil.

Daphne knows life can be hard and flesh will sometimes win but when she has to choose between HIS SECRETS or HER SANITY, this time, will she remain The Pastor's Admin?

https://www.amazon.com/dp/B07B9V4981

The Marriage Bed

Lynn and Jerome Watson have been together since meeting in the halls of Booker T. Washington High School, in 1993. Twenty-five years, a house, business and three children later they are on the heels of their 18th wedding anniversary and Lynn's 40th birthday. Her only request ... a night of fun, at home, with her husband and maybe a few toys.

Lynn thinks their marriage bed is suffering and wants to spice it up. Jerome, on the other hand, thinks Lynn is overreacting. His thoughts, if it ain't broke, don't break it trying to fix it. Then something happens that shakes up the Watson household and secrets are revealed but the biggest secret, Jerome has, and his lips are sealed.

https://www.amazon.com/dp/B07H51VS45

Still Fighting:

My sister's fight with Trigeminal Neuralgia

What would you do if you woke up one morning with pain doctors couldn't diagnose, medicine couldn't minimize, sleep couldn't stop and kept getting worse?

Still Fighting is an inside look into my sister's continued fight with Trigeminal Neuralgia, a condition known as the Suicide Disease because of the lives it has taken. In this book, I take you on a journey of recognition, route and restoration from my point of view; a sister who would stop at nothing to help her twin sister/best friend fight to live.

https://www.amazon.com/dp/B07MJHF6NL

The Forgotten Wife

All Rylee wants is her husband's attention.

She used to be the apple of Todd's eye but no matter what she did, lately, he was just too busy to notice her.

She could not help but wonder why.

Then one day, an unexpected email, subject line: Forgotten Wife and little did she know, it was about to play a major part in her life.

They say first comes love then comes ... a kidnapping, attacks, lies and affairs. Someone is out for blood but who, what, when and why?

Secrets are revealed and Rylee fears for her life, when all she ever wanted was not to be The Forgotten Wife.

https://www.amazon.com/gp/product/B07DRQ8NPR

Other Available Titles

A Compilation of Christian Stories: Box Set

Dear God: Hear My Prayer

2:32 AM: Losing My Faith in God

Chased

When the Vows Break 2

When the Vows Break 3

Tense

Shattered 2

Bible Chicks: Book 2

Doses of Devotion

You Only Live Once: Youth Devotional

HERoine Addict – Women's Journal

Be A Fighter – Journal

Surviving Me - Journal

CPSIA information can be obtained
at www.ICGtesting.com
Printed in the USA
LVHW081043300422
717484LV00014B/1419